NEMESIS
SINISTER INTENT

CATHERINE MacPHAIL

NEMESIS
SINISTER INTENT

BLOOMSBURY

First published in Great Britain in 2007 by Bloomsbury Publishing Plc
36 Soho Square, London, W1D 3QY

A CIP catalogue record of this book is available from the British Library

ISBN 978 0 7475 8270 0

All papers used by Bloomsbury Publishing are natural, recyclable products
made from wood grown in well-managed forests. The manufacturing
processes conform to the environmental regulations of the country of origin.

Typeset by Dorchester Typesetting Group Ltd
Printed in Great Britain by Clays Ltd, St Ives Plc

1 3 5 7 9 10 8 6 4 2

www.macphailbooks.com
www.bloomsbury.com

To Rebekah Helen

TUESDAY 2 A.M.

It was the lights I saw first, lights that illuminated the dark of the night. They appeared suddenly, bright and fierce. One second the pitch-black of night, and then the sky was ablaze with a light that almost blinded me.

At first I thought there had been some kind of explosion, but there had been no sound. Still was no sound.

No sound at all. Except for the thunderous rush of a nearby torrent of water. No birds, no hooting owls, no crickets or frogs. I began to get an eerie feeling that something was wrong.

So, step back, Ram, a voice whispered. The sensible part of me. But I wondered if I had ever been sensible. Had the memory that was lost to me ever done the sensible thing?

The beams were shining like searchlights in the night sky, somewhere over this hill. From the top, I was sure I would be able to see where that light came from, watch in safety and never be seen. Probably teenagers having a party. Nothing sinister at all. It would only take a moment to check it out. I lay flat and pulled myself up the steep slope, gripping at the grass and rocks, my feet scrabbling against earth and stone.

Still not a sound, just those bright lights.

I reached the top, dragging myself on my belly and cautiously peered over to see what was below in that valley.

Something was moving down there. Shapes that didn't look human. What had I stumbled on?

And then, in an instant, the light changed – from the bright white to a single green ray, shooting up out of the ground; a pencil of light beaming into the night sky. I leant closer, eager to see more – let loose some boulders at the top. The sound of the falling rocks roared into the silence as they rolled and crashed to the ground below.

The figures stood still. As one, they turned to where the sound was coming from, watching the rocks as they thundered to the ground. And that's when I saw the faces. I'd never seen anything like them. The faces weren't human, reflecting green from that strange light. Faces with no expressions, just blank stares.

I blinked. Now they were looking up. They were looking at me. Those inhuman faces were turned towards me. I felt the menace in those stares.

They began to move, as if some invisible force was sending them my way. They were coming closer, moving towards me. I wasn't going to wait for introductions. *Time to run, Ram.* I slithered on my belly down from the summit. Only got to my feet when I was sure I would be out of sight.

But I was only on my feet for a second. My foot caught on the roots of a tree and I pitched forward. I put my hands out to stop myself from falling, grabbing nothing but air. My hand cracked against stone. Down I tumbled, over and over, rocks slamming against my back, my shins, my face. At last I crashed to a stop.

I lay there; my head ached; I thought my heart was about to burst. I looked up. Something was caught in the light at the top of the hill. Something was moving there, seemed to shimmer in a green haze. One of them had reached the top. They were still after me. But I was sure they couldn't see me hidden here by bushes and trees. If I moved off into the darkness I would be safe. Unseen.

I tried to stand up, and the ground swayed and pitched beneath me as if there was an earthquake, but the earthquake was inside me.

I had to get away. I knew I had to get away. I took one step forward. The world turned upside down and the lights went out.

1

'Wake up, boy! Wake up!'

I was being shaken roughly. I opened my eyes and saw a host of strange faces staring down at me. Wild red hair, scarlet lips, and I remembered in that instant the beings I had seen – a moment ago? An hour ago? Or longer? How long had I been unconscious?

I scrambled back, away from those faces. That was when I realised just how much pain I was in. My head felt as if there was a bell clanging inside it. Every bone in my body ached. I was sure I was going to be sick.

'Are you all right?' a voice seemed to echo down a tunnel. 'Are you all right? Are you all right?'

The faces were merging now, from a legion of them to a dozen, to just a few. I shook my head, and the bell inside my head pealed out. Then I really was sick. I bent forward and vomited up over a pair of green brogue shoes.

And the thought came to me . . . is that what strange beings were wearing this year?

I looked up again. There was only one face now, vague and undefined. A hand still gripped tight at my shoulder.

'Are you all right, boy?' The voice was clear now.

It was an old woman who was leaning over me. It looked as if she had tried to dye her untamed hair and failed miserably. Strands of red stood up, embedded in grey roots. She was wearing lipstick. Unfortunately, it wasn't on her lips. She'd missed her lips by a mile and drawn a scarlet streak across her chin.

Who on earth was this?

'Can you stand up?' She was hauling me to my feet anyway. 'What are you doing out here this time of night? A boy your age?'

Same questions I was always asked. Still didn't have an answer.

'Never mind, you can tell me later.'

I tried to stand straight, but my legs wobbled like they were made of rubber. I would have crumpled to the ground if she hadn't held me.

'Lucky for you I've got transport,' she said, and she cackled. That was the only way to describe the laugh she let out. A cackle.

Oh no, I've come across another weirdo, I thought. Why was it always the weirdos who seemed to seek me out?

She helped me to sit again. 'You wait here. I'll be back in a minute,' she said.

I didn't want her to go. Weird as she was, she was human. Well, almost. And I didn't want to be alone. I imagined those things with their blank green faces, still watching, still waiting for the moment to come down and get me. But the old woman was gone before I had a chance to ask her to take me with her.

It was a still black night, deep black, heavy clouds hiding moon and stars. I looked up at the brow of the hill. No lights there now. No strange figures. No feeling of menace. The only sound the thunderous torrent of that nearby waterfall. Had it all been my imagination? Here in the dark of night, alone, had my imagination turned the headlights of a car into something sinister? Turned a couple of teenagers having a laugh into something menacing? Maybe it had been the headlights of the old woman's car I had seen. Maybe that was why she was here. If this was a strange place for a boy my age, it was an equally strange place for a little old lady to be in the middle of the night.

I heard her behind me, heard something trundling closer, and turned to look. It wasn't a car she had . . . it was a bike.

'What? That's your transport?'

'Oh, he's got a voice, and the first thing he does is complain.' She moved closer. 'I don't expect you to ride on the handlebars, don't worry. Look.' She turned the bike round. It had a little tent-like trailer hooked on to the back, the kind you might put a toddler in.

She was smiling. 'I usually put my shopping in here . . . in fact there might be a couple of potatoes still in there, but you can pop in. Save you walking.'

I tried to get to my feet. 'I'm not going in there.'

'What are you complaining about? I'm the one that's got to drag you behind me.'

I was feeling woozy again. She hurried towards me, caught me just before I fell. 'Come on, get in there. You need one of Bella's nice cups of tea.'

3

She pushed me in headfirst. I felt too sick to argue. Didn't fit inside either. My legs dangled out of the back.

She folded them in behind me. 'You're well hidden in there.' And then she said something that made me feel even sicker. 'There's people going missing around here . . . you're lucky I came when I did. You might have been one of them, eh?'

The Reaper was watching it all. It had only been a boy, of course, but it would have been better if they had caught him. He might have been useful. The old woman had come along too soon. Always in the way. One day she would be dealt with. The Reaper moved behind the bushes, careful not to make a sound, watching as she helped the boy up and on to his feet. Then she pushed him roughly inside the cart at the back of her bike.

Who was this boy? And what was he doing out here? And, most importantly, how much had he seen?

2

Her house was hidden somewhere inside an overgrown garden of weeds. I had expected some kind of ramshackle cottage, with smoke trailing from a chimney in the roof. But, actually, it was a modern house built on two storeys. She had just managed to make it look run-down. Had she said her name was Bella? I peered outside the cart as she bumped and grinded the bike over the broken slabs to her front door. I still felt woozy and sick, even sicker now. My head ached. I couldn't understand what was going on, but then, when did I ever understand anything?

It had only been days since I left the moors, and Faisal and Kirsten and Noel, sleeping rough in any place I could find. It amazed me the number of places a boy could find to sleep. A stone-built shed on the edge of a hill, a bothy, a hidden room, an abandoned house, a tunnel beside a long-forgotten station.

Now I was somewhere else, and I hadn't a clue where. All I could see from between the flaps in the cart was a modern estate laid out in a valley. The houses were in darkness. The streets were empty. Where was I?

One step ahead of the Dark Man – that was all that mattered.

The old woman, this Bella, hauled back the cover of the trailer. 'Right, let's get you inside.' She took my arm and almost lifted me out – strong, in spite of her age. She pushed open the back door of her house.

Why could I never meet normal people? A nice millionaire who was looking for a long-lost son? A beautiful rock star who wanted the publicity for adopting an orphan? What do I get? Some crazy old woman who talks in riddles and shoves me in the toddler cart at the back of her bike.

Inside her house was as untidy as her garden. She wiped a place clear on the settee for me to lie on, scattering papers and magazines on to the floor – along with a couple of long-haired cats, who didn't look too happy about being moved. 'That's Mata, and Hari, my lovely strays,' she said. 'Say hello to the nice boy.'

Mata and Hari only hissed at me. Mata was black and white. She looked as overgrown as Bella's garden, her coat standing out in tufts. Hari was a tortoiseshell with a half-shut eye. He looked as if he was winking at me.

'Now you lie there. I'll make you a cup of tea, and you can tell me all about yourself. I should introduce myself. My name's Bella Bartell.'

With that she disappeared into the kitchen. I could hear her clattering dishes about. *Maybe I should get out of here*, I thought. Now was my chance to escape. I tried to stand again, but it was no use. When I closed my eyes the room swirled. I had a pair of jelly legs. I sat back. Tell her about myself? What could I tell her? I had no memory of who I was. Or where I came from. All I knew was that a Dark Man, Mr Death, was on my trail, and my greatest fear was of him catching me. Yet I didn't know why he wanted me. What was the secret locked in my head? At the moment there didn't seem to be any room for any kind of secret, room for anything but this giant clanging bell.

'I think I'm going to be sick again,' I looked around for something to be sick into . . . even considered Mata and Hari's basket. They stared at me with narrowed eyes, daring me to use it.

The old woman came running in with a bucket. 'Here . . . be sick all you want. Enjoy.' So I was. But I can't say I enjoyed it.

I lay back on the settee. Sweat was pouring from me. My head was bursting with pain. I still felt sick. She touched my brow. 'I think I'm going to get the doctor,' she said.

I was up in the instant she said it. 'No! I'm fine. Please don't.'

A doctor. Publicity. The Dark Man finding me again. Couldn't risk it.

She sat beside me, shook her head. 'Oh . . . a boy with a secret, eh? Don't want to be caught. Run away, have you? Wondered what you were doing up there. Strange place for a boy to be in the middle of the night . . . unless he's up to no good. *Have* you run away?'

I didn't know what to say to that. I didn't have to bother saying anything. She seemed happy supplying the answers for herself. 'Had a bad time at home, did you? So many young people run away because of that.

Don't want anybody to know you're here, is that it?'

I nodded weakly, and the bell rang loudly inside my head, swaying from side to side in slow motion. Beating against my temples.

'I quite understand,' she said. She stood up. 'And I promise I won't give you away. But I am going to send for the doctor. Don't worry. Dr Mulvey's a friend, and I won't tell him anything. I'll make up a story about you. About why you're here. Now what's your name?'

How could I tell her I didn't know that either. I had a made-up name that I had plucked from thin air . . . Or had I?

Ram. Did my name mean something?

She leant down to me. 'Not normally a hard question. Your name . . . What do you want me to call you, then?'

'Ram,' I said. 'Just call me Ram.'

She didn't make any comment on that. 'How would it be if I adopted you for a bit? I'll say you're my grandson come for a visit. He'll believe that. Nobody really knows me very well here. They all think I'm mad as a hatter. But then, everybody's as mad as a hatter in this town. This is the UFO capital of the UK. Did you know that?'

'UFO?' I mumbled, puzzled. What did that mean?

'Unidentified flying objects,' she explained. 'Spaceships. Little green men from Mars.'

I let out a gasp. She caught it, must have seen the expression on my face.

'Oh, don't say you've seen something as well? Is that what happened back there in the valley?' She tutted. 'It was your imagination. Listen, we've got enough trouble in this world without importing it from outer space.' She leant down to me. 'There's certainly something going on here, but it's got nothing to do with spaceships.'

I was too weak to argue. All I wanted to do was sleep, but she wouldn't let me. 'Not till the doctor comes,' she said. 'You might have concussion.'

She poured me a mug of tea from a cat-shaped teapot, and handed it to me. 'Maybe you'll be able to keep that down.' I looked at the tea. There were a couple of grey hairs streaked with red floating in it. She didn't even blush. 'They're not mine, you know,' she insisted. 'Either Mata or Hari. Their hairs get everywhere. Just pick them out.'

I didn't manage to keep the tea down after all.

3

I lay on the sofa, shivering, while she busied herself in the kitchen. I heard her switch on the radio and night music from a local station filled the air. I wanted to get up and walk out, move back into the shadows where I was safe. But I was too weak. Once the headache left me, then I could go.

The music faded and the news came on. The cheery voice of the presenter seemed at odds with the dark news. The terrorist threat. The lone bomber. Hostages held by a foreign power. His voice almost became a giggle as he began talking about the next item.

'And now for one of our Mad March stories. In a small sleepy town not far from here a woman has been claiming her nephew isn't her nephew, but a ghost sent to haunt her. How does she know this? Because she claims she murdered her nephew.' I sat up. He was talking about Noel Christie. Had to be. The presenter was almost laughing. 'She even told the police where to find the nephew's body. Wasn't there, of course, and the nephew is undoubtedly who he says he is, as DNA tests have confirmed. But she still insists he's a ghost. This story, by the way, comes from the same area where there have been sightings of some sort of wild beast roaming the countryside – probably reported by the same woman! Or maybe there's something in the water up there. Well, if you have any more Mad March stories out there, let us know. Though this one will take a lot to beat.'

The story was about Noel. The boy I had replaced, who now had taken his rightful place. Our plan had worked. Noel was safe.

I was feeling a mite cheerier by the time the doctor arrived. He looked as if he should have retired many moons ago. Grey hair, what he had of it and a face lined like old leather. He shuffled into the room, with Bella just behind him. I noticed she had put on more lipstick, still missing her lips. It made me think that maybe she fancied him. She was certainly fluttering her eyelashes at him.

'So is this another of your strays, Bella?' he asked. He smiled at me. 'Bella picks up strays all the time.'

'No, he's my grandson, Dr Mulvey. I told you on the phone.'

'Your grandson?' the doctor said, as if he didn't believe her. 'Didn't know you had any family. You never mentioned him before.'

'Oh, well, you know me – keep myself to myself. There's only the one grandson. He's arrived tonight. I just picked him up.'

Picked me up indeed. Now that wasn't any lie.

'But he fell down my stairs,' she went on. 'He's very clumsy on his feet, and he's not been feeling right since.'

Dr Mulvey placed his hand on my brow. 'Bit of a

temperature,' he said. He eased himself on to a chair beside me and took his stethoscope out of his case. 'Let's have a listen . . . Heart beating like a drum,' he said after a few moments. 'Healthy boy.'

'He's been sick,' Bella said.

'Headache?' the doctor asked. I almost told him just how bad the headache was but he turned to Bella just then. 'Maybe we should get him to the hospital and have him checked out.'

That was the last thing I wanted. I took a deep breath. 'No. No headache at all. Don't even feel sick now.'

I just hoped I didn't make myself out a liar by vomiting all over him.

He checked my eyes and my pulse, gripped my head in his hands and moved it up and down, from right to left. I felt myself going woozy again.

Finally, he was finished. He looked up at Bella. 'Get him into bed. Nothing broken, no lasting damage.' He laughed. 'Sure you didn't get me here for ulterior motives, Bella?'

Bella blushed the same colour as her lipstick. 'You're a devil, Dr Mulvey.'

Dr Mulvey smiled too. He stood up. 'Well, it's nice meeting you, young man. I'll pop in tomorrow, see how you are.'

Pop in all you want, I thought. *I have no intention of being here tomorrow.*

I could hear them whispering at the door. Whispering sweet nothings probably.

Bella came back a few minutes later. The doctor's car purred away from the house. 'Isn't he dishy?' she said.

I tried to sit up. 'Dishy? He's as old as the hills.'

'He's not that old. He's a lot younger than me. He's my toy boy.'

'Toy boy! He looks ancient.'

'He just hasn't worn well.' She nodded and laughed. 'It's a race against time who gets me first. Him or the Grim Reaper.' Then she cackled again.

Her voice went right through me. 'OK, that's our cover story. While you're here I'll say you're my grandson,' she went on. 'And I've told him your name is Ramon.'

'Ramon?' What was the idea of that? 'Where did you get that name?'

'It's close enough to your own name . . . and it reminds me of my mother's favourite movie star. Ramon Navarro.'

'I don't believe you. Nobody was ever called Ramon Navarro.'

She waved over to a computer that sat in the corner. I hadn't noticed it before, covered with coats and towels and with either Mata or Hari slumped on top of it. 'You look it up on my computer. You'll find out all about Ramon Navarro. So you're called after him.'

'Have you a grandson?'

'No. No family at all. Never had time to have one. I was a career woman.' She waited as if I was supposed to ask her what her career had been, but I said nothing. 'No grandson. No family. I'm all alone in the world.' If she said that to get my sympathy she was barking up the wrong grandson. I think she did the world a favour. This woman was nuts.

13

'Anyway, what you need now is bed. You'll feel better in the morning.'

She lifted me by the arm and helped me up the stairs to a small landing where there were two bedrooms. She flung open the door of one of them. It was jammed pack full of old furniture, black bin bags and boxes. 'Is this the junk room?' I asked.

'You cheeky monkey! It's my guest bedroom. It just needs a little feng shui.' She looked closer. 'There's a bed in here somewhere.'

And she wasn't lying. We finally found the bed under a pile of boxes and bags and second-hand clothes. Bella shook the dust from the duvet, pulled back the covers. 'There,' she said. 'You'll sleep great in there.'

A second later Mata and Hari bounded up the stairs and threw themselves on the bed before I had a chance to move. Bella grinned. 'There's plenty of room for the three of you.'

It was only as I lay on the edge of the bed – Mata and Hari took up most of the room – that I began thinking again about the place where I had seen the lights. I had forgotten to ask what exactly Bella Bartell had been doing there in the middle of the night. Had she seen them too? The lights, and those strange figures with their non-human faces?

The UFO capital of the UK, she had said. People going missing. What had I stumbled into now?

4

I awoke later to go to the toilet. As soon as I moved, Mata and Hari rolled into my place. I had a feeling I would have to fight to get it back. I opened the door, ready to creep down the stairs. Bella would surely be snoring noisily in her bed by now.

But she wasn't.

Halfway down the stairs I could see a green light in the living room. Otherwise the house was in darkness. I could hear the gentle touch of fingers flying over keys. The door was slightly ajar. I peered closer. Bella Bartell was on her computer. She didn't look dotty or forgetful at all now. She was sitting up straight and looked as sharp as a knife. She seemed intent on the screen in front of her. She had told me she had no family. She was all alone in the world, but she certainly had someone to send emails to. I stepped back. Something strange was going on here, I was sure of it. But what?

After I'd gone back upstairs, I stood at the window in the bedroom, wondering if I should go right now, get away from here. I had a gut instinct that would be the wise thing to do. I was safer keeping on the move. But my head still ached. My legs were shaking. The pull of that warm bed, even sharing it with two scruffy cats, was too hard to resist. If I could get back some strength I would be fit to move on, I told myself. Maybe tomorrow. Maybe then I would go.

I pulled back the curtains and peered outside. Mist from the drizzly rain hung over the houses like smoke. From this window I could see the town laid out below. The houses were in darkness, only the street lights illuminated the night. People asleep. Then I turned my eyes to the hills. Total darkness there. No strange lights now. Nothing.

I would definitely leave tomorrow, I decided. Bella Bartell was an old woman. But there was something not quite right about her, and I wasn't hanging around to find out what it was.

The Reaper had been right. It *was* the boy he had seen at the site. He could see him at the window now, watching. His face thoughtful and troubled. What had he been doing there in the valley? Did he understand what he had been looking at? Who would believe him anyway? No point stirring up any suspicions. The boy might just move on. That would solve everything. But if he didn't . . . well, he knew exactly what he could do with a nosy young boy.

Someone else was at a window, watching everything through a pair of high-powered binoculars. Ryan Gallacher, boy detective. He had been investigating

16

Bella Bartell for a long time. There was something strange about her. She was always behaving suspiciously, riding about the town on that old bike of hers, her wild hair flying behind her.

It was the doctor's car driving past his house that had woken Ryan. Why was the doctor here in the middle of the night? (If Dr Mulvey really was a doctor! His dad had said he should have been struck off years ago. Though struck off what, Ryan hadn't understood.) Anyway, he had watched him going into Bella Bartell's house, and waited until he came back out, clutching his case. Then he watched him drive off.

Ryan wondered at first if Bella Bartell was ill. Or maybe dead. She was certainly old enough. But now he could see a boy standing at the upstairs window, holding back the net curtain, looking outside. A boy about his own age. A boy he had never seen before. Dark hair, long pale face. He looked ill, or maybe that was fear? Was Bella Bartell keeping him in there against his wishes? He drew out his notebook, made some entries quickly. Tomorrow he was going to investigate further.

I climbed back into bed with the two cats. They refused to budge. Eventually I managed to balance myself on the edge of the bed and hold on tight. It was like clinging to the side of a mountain. I was trying to force myself not to be sick. I would not be sick. I wanted so much to feel well again. But my head reeled. I was sweating buckets. Had she given me something to make me feel like this? I mean, what did I know about this old woman? I needed

17

to leave. If I could just stand up. If my legs would only support me.

I imagined myself standing erect, walking out of the room, down the stairs, striding out of the front door and off into the night. It all seemed so real I was sure I had done it, that I would open my eyes and find myself outside in the open air. But when I did open my eyes, Hari was staring at me with his one good eye. I was still in the bed in Bella's spare room. Eventually, I gave up even trying. I closed my eyes and, moments later, I was fast asleep.

5

It was birdsong that woke me. What kind of bird I couldn't tell, but it sure made one awful noise. I sat up. My head still ached. I clutched at it to stop that bell from clanging. As soon as I sat up so did the two cats, leaping out of the bed and heading for the door. I had to admire their ingenuity as they pawed at the bottom of the door and eventually pulled it open. Then Mata turned her green eyes on me, as if to say, 'Coming?' So I did.

I followed them downstairs, padding as softly as they did. All was quiet. The computer in the living room was switched off and covered once again by clothes and blankets, as if it was never used. Why would Bella Bartell try to hide the fact that she used her computer?

She was nowhere about. I crept into the kitchen, looking for food. Suddenly, the two cats decided they liked me. They wound themselves round my legs, purring. Never trust a cat, I thought. They wouldn't give me an inch of the bed all night. I was sure given the right circumstances they would scratch my eyes out. Yet here they were as if we were best pals. I pulled open the fridge door. The milk was past its sell-by date. So was the cheese by the look of the green coating. I moved it aside.

There was an unopened pack of gammon. I lifted it out and looked around for some bread.

Was Bella Bartell still sleeping? I wondered as I munched into the bread. It was definitely not fresh, but I was too hungry to care. Here was my chance to go. I still didn't feel too well, the headache was killing me. But I had the chance to leave and I was going to take it. I looked round for my coat, Jake's coat, and there it was, lying in a heap on the settee. Did this woman never hang things up? I pulled it on, and as quietly as I could I opened the front door.

It was still dark. Still raining. There would be no sunrise this morning. The sun was well hidden behind a heavy curtain of clouds. I trod softly up her garden path and was almost out of her gate when a boy suddenly leapt out in front of me – took me so much by surprise I nearly fell over. He grabbed me by the arm and hauled me back into the jungle that overflowed from Bella's garden.

'Who are you?' I pulled myself away from him, ready to run.

He had dark hair cut really short, but with hints of blond through it. Like it was the fashion or something.

'Who am I? Who are you?' was his answer. 'How did you get here? Has she kidnapped you? I saw you at her window last night. You looked scared. Are you in danger?'

'At the moment the only person I'm in danger from is you.' I stepped back from him. 'What's your game?'

He grinned at me. 'I'm investigating Bella Bartell,' he said. He pulled a notebook from his pocket. 'I'm Ryan,

Ryan Gallacher. I live over there.' He pointed past Bella's overgrown hedge towards a large detached house. 'I've been watching her for a while. She's a very strange woman.'

Tell me about it, I thought.

He flicked through the pages of the notebook. 'I've got so many facts here. She's always at the police, telling them people are going missing here. Nobody listens to her. But she's actually right. People are going missing round here. Thing is, I think she's the one who's taking them. I think she might be an alien.'

Another nutcase. An alien! If he had said she might have escaped from the local nuthouse, there's a chance I'd have believed him. But an alien!

'An alien? What makes you think that?'

'She's definitely got a secret. She behaves very suspiciously. Makes friends with the weirdest people.' He blinked when he realised he might be referring to me. 'Present company excepted. Anyway, I mean to find out what it is she's hiding.'

Then I remembered Bella at the computer during the night. The daft old woman. Was this boy right? Was she hiding something? Why did I care? I just wanted away.

He began to whisper. 'Where did she come from? Nobody knows. Nobody knows anything about her. She moved in here just a couple of years ago. Nobody knows anything about her past.' He paused and peered at me closely. 'You look ill.'

'Just a fever,' I answered.

'I heard my dad say Bella Bartell's one for the watching,' Ryan said. 'So I'm watching her. And this is the

21

UFO capital of the country.' He told me that proudly. 'Did you know that?'

I saw again in my mind the green light, the blank faces, the strange figures. 'Yes, she told me.'

The boy grinned. I realised that this was obviously his favourite subject. 'It's a great place to live. There's always sightings of UFOs here. I've seen strange things in the sky. Up in the valley.' He stopped to take a breath then hurried on. 'There's been rumours of a government cover-up. They say the truth is that aliens really did land here years ago and the government doesn't want anyone to know about it. And I think that Bella Bartell is one of them.'

I must have looked as if I didn't believe him.

'Honest. It's true.' He dared me to contradict him. 'Everyone has an alien story in this town. We even have someone who claims the aliens took him, and then brought him back.' He shrugged that away. 'He's only daft Lenny though. No wonder they brought him back. He's not dealing with a full pack.' He began to giggle. 'Or a full set of fingers. He's lost three of them.'

I couldn't see that was anything to laugh about.

'He says the aliens took them,' Ryan went on.

He looked again at me. 'And he's one of her weird friends too. He goes in there and she feeds him. I think if we're not careful they're all going to gang up on us. Get together and attack us. So, are you going to tell me who you are?'

And what was I to say? Who was I? A boy with no memory and a Dark Man on my trail. A boy who couldn't risk anyone finding out about me, till that secret I had locked in my memory burst to the surface.

He was still looking at me. He began to laugh. 'Is it a hard question?' He seemed to think I wasn't answering because I didn't feel well. 'You look awful. I saw the doctor here last night. Old Dr Mulvey. He's weird as well. Keeps his Christmas lights on all year round. He even keeps a Santa and his sleigh lit up on his roof.'

'That sounds pretty harmless,' I said.

'Hardly anybody else in the town goes to Dr Mulvey except her.'

Another of Bella's strays, I thought. I wondered if there was anyone who wasn't weird in this town.

'You really do look pale.' He peered closer as if he expected me to keel over at any moment. 'Who are you?'

'He's my blinkin' grandson, and his name's Ramon, you nosy little devil!' It was Bella, rushing through the jungle of her garden, a coat wrapped round her, her pyjamas underneath. 'What are you doing here, Ryan Gallacher?'

The boy, Ryan, looked paler than me then. He stood rigid in front of her. 'I'm sorry. I thought he was sick.'

'He is sick; he shouldn't be outside.' She looked at me. She still had the lipstick on, as if she never went outside without it. Pity it still wasn't on her lips. 'You get back in that house, young man. The doctor's coming back to see you.' She began waving her arms about at Ryan. 'And as for you, off you go. Off my property. I've told you before what I'll do to trespassers.'

She stamped her feet as if she was about to chase him. I'm sure Ryan had never run so fast. Bella had me by the

23

sleeve to stop me running off too. 'I was just going to move on,' I said softly. 'I'm fine now.'

She began to drag me back to the house. 'Nonsense. You're white as a milk bottle. You need a couple of days rest. And believe me . . . you're safer with me, than let loose in this town.'

6

When the doctor came I was going to ask for help. This old dear was crazy. Maybe she was harmless, but she was definitely crazy. She dragged me back into the house and pinned me down under her two cats.

'I think they've taken to you, Ramon,' she said.

'Why are you keeping me here?'

She ignored the question and put a gooey grey mess in front of me. I thought it was for the cats. Their litter tray probably. 'Porridge,' she assured me. 'Now eat up; it's good for you.'

I would have to be force-fed this goo. Even the cats sniffed and turned away from it. 'You haven't answered my question,' I said.

She turned to face me then. 'And you haven't answered mine. Who are you?'

It was at moments like these she wasn't this daft old woman who had rescued me. She seemed sharp as a butcher's knife. I rubbed at my forehead. 'I think that fall gave me temporary amnesia.' I shook my head as if I was trying to shake the memory back in. 'Nope. Can't remember a thing.'

She sat down at the table across from me. 'Temporary

amnesia. It's very common after some kind of trauma. Have you had some kind of trauma recently?'

'I told you, last night . . . the fall.'

She waved that away as if it was cigarette smoke. 'Rubbish. You don't get amnesia rolling down a hill. Something major's happened to you and you've lost your memory.'

'Something major,' I repeated. 'But I don't know what.'

'Anyone looking for you?' she asked.

'Bound to be,' I lied. For I had looked on websites, searched the internet, and found nothing about me. No one cared. No one was looking for me – except the Dark Man.

I pushed the cats off my lap, stood up. 'Ryan thinks you're an alien.'

That made her laugh. 'That boy is obsessed with aliens. But like I said, there may be strange things going on around here, but they're nothing to do with UFOs.'

'Last night you said people were going missing?'

'And they are, but I can't get anybody to listen to me. Young girl goes missing . . . they say she fell out with her boyfriend, ran off. Even her family think that. Man goes missing. Turns out he'd embezzled money from his firm. Woman goes missing. She'd been running about with the butcher. And then the butcher goes missing as well. So they say they've run off together.'

It all sounded logical to me. 'Maybe they did.'

'I know when something weird is going on.' She ran a hand up the back of her neck. 'I can always feel it here. Can't get anybody to listen. I'm too old. They think I'm

26

losing it.' She went on almost as if I wasn't there. 'Didn't always think like that. People used to listen to Bella Bartell. Her information was important.'

'Look, I'll be on my way. You've got enough to handle round here. Thank you for all your trouble.'

'You're not going anywhere. You need somewhere safe to rest for a few days. Stay here. I'll look after you.' Her watery blue eyes narrowed. She peered at me. 'You might not be able to remember . . . but you're frightened of something . . . or someone.'

'Maybe that's why I have to move on. Don't want that someone to find me.'

'I can understand that. But you're not well, son. I'd feel guilty letting you go off when you're like this.'

I thought of what Ryan had said and I asked her straight out. 'Are you trying to keep me here against my will?' The very thought of that, of course, was ridiculous. She was small, frail and thin. One shove and I could have her on the floor . . . and I thought, not for the first time, that I wasn't a bad boy, a villain. I must have been brought up right. Because I would never do that.

'No, son, you're free to go any time you want.' She stepped over to the back door and held it open. 'Here. Go. Go on. I'll not stop you.'

Here was my chance. I moved forward, ready to do just that. And the room began to spin. Bella became two. She was right. I still wasn't well. I sat down again. 'I'm going tomorrow,' I said with determination. 'I'll feel better tomorrow.'

That seemed to please her. 'A couple of days' rest and

27

good feeding and you'll be ready for anything.'

I glanced, again at the grey congealing mess on the table. I'd be more likely to lose weight after a couple of days here.

Her eyes lost that sharpness. She put on her dotty old woman look. 'You've made an old woman very happy. Just for a few days I'm going to have a grandson. My little Ramon. No one will ask any questions about my grandson staying with me, will they? You'll be safe here from whoever's after you.'

'Ryan. Where on earth have you been?' His mother picked bits of grass and bush out of his blazer. 'You can't go to school looking like that. You look as if you've been dragged through a hedge backwards.' Ryan blushed. His mother had hit the nail on the head. He almost had been dragged through Bella Bartell's hedge backwards. Ryan tried to think up something fast. Detectives should do that: always have a cover story ready. Not fast enough for his mum.

'Have you been spying again? I found your dad's binoculars up in your room.'

His dad tutted. 'Not that silly old woman in the next house?'

'I don't think she's so silly, Dad,' Ryan said. His dad didn't look convinced. 'I think she's got a secret.'

'And what do you think her secret is?' his dad asked.

Ryan wanted to say he thought she was an alien, some kind of evil alien. But who would ever believe that? They'd think he was crazy. So instead he said, 'I think

28

she's a criminal.'

His mother laughed. 'At least you don't think she's an alien. That makes a change. I love this town: everyone here has either been abducted at some time or is waiting to go back to their home planet.'

But it was true, Ryan wanted to say. He had seen lights at night, strange green lights. His dad said they were probably planes. They were close to the airport – that was where his mum and dad worked. Or else, his dad told him, they might just be car headlights, reaching into the night. And Ryan knew that wasn't so. There was something funny going on in this town. Why wouldn't anyone believe him? And he hated to admit agreeing with Bella Bartell, but people were going missing. He had noticed it too.

'Well, I don't want you going anywhere near her house from now on,' his mother said.

'But I met her grandson,' Ryan said and his dad popped his head up from behind his paper.

'She has a grandson?'

'His name's Ramon,'

'Ramon!' His dad raised an eyebrow at his mum. 'She would have to have a grandson with a fancy foreign name.'

'Honest, Dad, he's perfectly normal . . . like us. He was nice, but I think he's sick or something. The doctor came to see him in the middle of the night. Dr Mulvey.' He said it mysteriously, wanting his dad to think, like him, that something sinister was going on if Dr Mulvey was part of it. His dad only went back to his paper. 'He's definitely sick,' Ryan said.

'Well, just you keep back from him. It might be catching,' his mother said.

But Ryan couldn't do that. There was a mystery here, a mystery about Bella, and maybe if he made friends with Ramon, he might just discover what her secret was.

7

By the afternoon I woke up and felt better. My headache had gone. I could hear Bella moving about in the room below then begin to climb the stairs. I closed my eyes, pretending I was still asleep. I heard the door creak open, could sense her watching me. Then she closed the door quietly and went downstairs. It was late afternoon; the sky was dark; heavy clouds hung over the hills. I heard her talking to her cats, telling them to look after the house while she was out. As if she could trust *them*. They would let in anyone who would feed them.

When I was sure she had left the house, I got up out of bed. From the window I watched her wobble off on her bike, heading down towards the town. Now was my chance to go, and this time she wasn't here to stop me.

I dressed quickly and went downstairs. *I shouldn't be doing this*, I thought. I still didn't feel a hundred per cent. Bella was right. I did need rest. But I didn't feel safe here. I was sure I wasn't far enough away from the Dark Man. It was time for me to go.

Bella would understand. She would come back and find me gone, and she would understand. She could make up some story to the doctor that I was needed at home.

I didn't even take food. The very thought of food made me feel ill. I looked at myself in the mirror in Bella's kitchen. My face looked wan and thin, my eyes seemed to be sunk into smoky black hollows. There were little beads of sweat on my upper lip. 'Go back to bed,' I said aloud. And I longed to.

But the voice inside me answered. 'No chance. Go. Stay safe.'

I pulled open the front door. The drizzle had turned to hammering rain. I would be soaked in five minutes. But I would only be wet for a while; I comforted myself with that thought. I would find somewhere warm and dry tonight. Didn't I always? And I began to walk.

I left the road and took the forest path up behind the town. I always felt safer away from the main roads. From this vantage point at the top of the hill, I took a minute to stop under the dubious shelter of a tree and look down at the town laid before me. Everything was grey, heavy clouds hung low, mist trailed through the streets. A funny town, I thought. No shops, no centre, no heart. Only houses. Just a place for people to sleep, it seemed to me.

I turned and began to walk on. I could feel the dampness soak through to my back. I was burning up. Wasn't thinking of where I was going, just away from this town. Yet suddenly I realised where I was heading: back to the place where Bella had found me. It was the wild thunder of water that alerted me. It sounded even fiercer with the driving rain. Maybe it was good I was leaving the town this way. Going back towards that valley, assuring myself that there was nothing mysterious about it.

There was no uncanny silence today. Sounds were shrieking into the air, almost lost in the fury of the waterfall. Inhuman, high-pitched screams. I imagined the figures I had seen, standing somewhere behind the rise, waiting for me. The thought of them scared me. *Leave this place, turn away*. I even took a few steps back, but I stopped when I began to make out what the sounds were. Nothing inhuman at all. They were boys' voices, taunting someone.

'Go on, in you go! Come on, ya big daft boy, you're not scared, are you?'

There was a strangled, frightened yell. Someone sounded terrified. I began to run towards the sound.

As I came through some trees I saw them. A bunch of boys, crowding round a man – at least he was the size of a man. His big hands were clamped over his ears. I couldn't not notice those hands. Three fingers missing on one of them. This must be Lenny – the boy Ryan had told me about. He was moaning, trying to get away from the boys, but they surrounded him, circled him, pushing him this way and that. They were screaming like hyenas. It was that sound that seemed to be freaking Lenny out. I'd never seen such terror in anyone's face.

He was a big, powerful man, but his face was like a child's and at this moment, a frightened child. The boys were backing him against the edge of the water. For the first time I saw the waterfall. Lenny and his tormentors were silhouetted against its fierce spray. It gushed from somewhere inside the hills, then seemed to plunge almost vertically down and disappear into a black hole in the earth below. It looked terrifying.

I could see that with just a few more steps Lenny could tumble down there. I let out a yell of my own. 'Stop!'

They all turned. I saw Lenny stumble and just manage to keep his balance. They all had a hold of him, a painful hold of his arms, of his legs. Why didn't he kick out and free himself? He looked strong enough.

One of the boys yelled back, 'What's your problem?'

'What are you doing?' I shouted, my voice almost lost in the sound of the fierce water. 'Stop!'

'You goin' to make us?'

I didn't answer that. I made a sudden rush at them. I tried to pull Lenny away from them. 'Leave him be.'

One of the boys did just that. He let Lenny go and reached out to punch me. I fell back and his fist hit air. But I kept my feet.

'What are you sticking up for daft Lenny for?'

One of the others spoke. 'He's going down Dobie's Doom, that right, Lenny?' And with that Lenny screeched as he was given another push.

Dobie's Doom. Was that what they called it? I looked at the rollercoaster of water that plunged straight down. I took a step back from it. They couldn't be serious. Once in that water there was no other place to go but down. They would never surely do that to another human being? Thing was, they didn't seem to think Lenny *was* a human being.

I suddenly grabbed at Lenny, and, with all the strength I had, pulled him towards me. It took them by surprise and Lenny almost fell on top of me. He was shaking, rain dripping from his face – might have been tears.

I rolled away, but I had only made this crowd mad. Suddenly, they turned their fury on me. Lenny stumbled back, glad not to be their target. I tried to get up but first one grabbed me, then the other. They had me. They pulled me to my feet.

'So, you don't want Lenny to go down Dobie's Doom . . . OK, you're the boss.' He looked round at the others. They were all grinning. 'What about you?' he said to me. 'Are you willing to take his place?'

They dragged me to the edge of the waterfall. I dug my heels into the mud, but there was no hold there. I yelled, but the savage sound of that water blotted out any other. I struggled, but there were way too many of them. I tried not to look down, but two of the boys forced my head round so I had to see. See where the falls would take me. Down into nothing.

Down into a black hole.

8

Bella watched the clock. The boy was gone. She should never have left him. She could have picked up clothes for him at the charity shop another day. Any other day. He needed looking after. He still wasn't well enough to be on the road. Why did he feel he had to go? What was the urgency that was driving him on? What was the boy's secret? Who was he so afraid of? He was no ordinary runaway, of that she was sure.

He wouldn't come back now. Part of her wanted to go out and look for him, sure she would find him unconscious in a ditch somewhere. Another voice inside her said, *Let him go*. Perhaps he was safer away from this town. He seemed to be able to take care of himself anyway. There were too many strange things going on here.

Now someone else had gone missing. The girl who worked at the charity shop. She hadn't been in for the past two days, but everyone assumed she had just moved on. She'd been waiting for word about a permanent job in London, they told her. Probably got the job and moved on without telling them. She was an inconsiderate young woman, the starched lady behind the counter had informed Bella. But Bella considered that young girl to be another of the missing. And what could she do about it? She felt useless and stupid. There was no point even going to the police. They were fed up with her 'stories'. No one listened to her any more.

My feet were slipping on the wet pebbles at the edge of the falls. I tried to cling on to one of the boy's coats, but he plucked my fingers from it and held me further over the water. Stones scattered under my feet and I watched them splash into the foam and disappear into the mouth of the black hole. Now I was only held by my coat. They pulled me back and forth, laughing at me, shaking me. If one let me go, then another, I was done for.

'You can't do this!' I yelled. 'You can't.'

'Give us one good reason why not? Who's goin' to know? Once you're gone, you're gone. No proof.'

Why had I come back here? Where did that black hole go? Pitch-blackness down inside there. I let out a yell as I slipped again. My feet were touching the water now, ice-cold water gushing and churning; a foot lower and the current would surely pull me out of their grasp. No escape! Why was this happening to me? If I went, who would miss me? Nobody. Bella would only think I had run off again. Would she inform the police, tell them I might be another of those missing persons? In those terrifying moments I knew she wouldn't.

I didn't want to die and no one miss me. No one care. They were going to let me go and I couldn't do anything about it. The grass was sliding under my feet. I was losing my balance. Going down. I began to shake. My mind was a tumble of short memories. Gaby and Zoe and Jake, and Faisal and Kirsten and Noel . . . and the Dark Man. I could almost see his face, his smile as if he was watching me, watching all this happening. I tried to shake the thought of him away. Didn't want my last conscious memory to be of him, my enemy.

My life was flashing before me – was that what was happening to me now? Wouldn't take long. I didn't have much of a life to remember. I yelled again, and it seemed my voice echoed into emptiness. Only one person to help me and that was this Lenny, and he was shivering under a rock, his hands still clamped over his ears, just watching.

Another of them released his grip on me with a wild yell. Now there were only two of them holding me. And they were smiling malevolently, ready to let me go at any moment.

'NOOOOO!' I screamed it out.

My only hope was Lenny.

9

It was a roar I heard, like the roar of a wild beast. They all turned to look. I opened my eyes, sure it must be Lenny, racing to my rescue.

But it wasn't.

When the gang saw what was charging towards them they really did let me go. My arms flailed wildly, I was sure I was going down. I screamed. And someone was suddenly gripping my arms firmly, pulling me back from the edge. One hand on my coat, the other grabbing at my hair. It hurt like hell but I didn't care. Then it was my shoulders. Firm hands holding me fast. I began to help myself, pushing at the stones, my feet still slipping as if I was on ice, but I was pushing myself forward. The edge of the waterfall and the long drop into that black mouth disappeared from view. I was dragged on to the bank, shaking.

The boys were off. I watched them running, one of them rolling down the hill in his hurry to get away. Even Lenny was running with them, as if whoever had saved me scared him too. I coughed and spluttered, began to shake even more as the cold and the damp penetrated my clothes.

'Here, son, cough it up. Bad water there, bad.' The voice was a man's. At last I looked at him, saw him clearly and couldn't believe what I was seeing. He looked like some kind of wild man. Grey matted hair, a beard like a bird's nest, his teeth broken and brown. But the eyes were sharp and clear and blue with tiny flecks of grey through them.

'Bad water?' I spluttered the words out.

'Comes from in there.' He nodded towards the hill. 'The hills are hollow,' he said mysteriously. 'Bad water,' he said again.

I sat up, shivering so badly my teeth chattered, cold and fear taking hold of me. I looked down at the waterfall as it tumbled and gushed down towards the black hole. 'Where does it go?' I asked.

He was still staring at it. 'Down to hell,' he said, as if he knew exactly what hell looked like.

'Thanks, I thought I was a goner there.'

He turned his eyes on me, bright eyes that looked as if they didn't belong in that weather-beaten, life-scarred face. Yet, in spite of their sharpness there was a look of despair in them. 'You would have been. Bunch of bad boys, them. Wouldn't put it past them to have let you go. What were they doing? Tormenting poor Lenny?'

'They were shouting at him. Screaming at him. And he was terrified. What's wrong with him?'

'It's the shouting. He hates it. Can't handle it. He's terrified of noise – screaming, yelling. They know that. Lenny, the local daft boy. Says he was abducted by aliens and that was the noise they make when they talk,

40

screaming in a high-pitched whine. Did you know he was abducted?'

He watched me as he said it, waiting for my reaction. 'Hasn't everybody around here?' I said.

He smiled. 'In this town . . . probably. Well, whatever's up there,' he nodded towards the sky, 'can't be any worse than what's here already. World's full of evil,' he said bitterly.

'There's lots of good too,' I muttered. After all, he'd come and saved me, hadn't he?

He lifted a bushy eyebrow. 'You can say that after what they tried to do to you? The world's getting worse,' he said and he spat on the ground as if the world gave him a bad taste in his mouth. And I wondered what had happened to him to make him so bitter.

Change the subject, Ram, I told myself. *None of my business what his story is.* 'They called it Dobie's Doom,' I said.

He grinned. The grime on his face lined the wrinkles. His whole face spoke of a hard life on the road. If I stayed on the run, would I look like him one day? 'This place has always had a bad reputation,' he answered. 'They say the ancient tribes used it for human sacrifices, the witches too. Casting spells. When someone was accused of witchcraft, this was their punishment. The villagers would drop some poor old woman into the Doom and if she managed to get herself out they decided she must be a witch and they burnt her to death, and if she didn't . . . well, then they realised the poor old soul must be innocent, so they prayed for her. The human race hasn't learnt too much since then, eh? We're still

41

killing the innocents.'

I looked down at that black hole, tried to think how terrifying it must have been to know no matter what happened you were going to die anyway.

'Who was Dobie?' I asked.

'First man recorded in the town records who was ever thrown down there. Children had been going missing in the area. He was the prime suspect. The villagers decided to take the law into their own hands. They dragged him up here . . . on a day just like this.'

The rain was coming down like steel rods. The sky was a leaden grey. A bad day to die, I thought.

'Doom's always roaring in weather like this,' he went on. 'They say Dobie screamed something awful, screaming his innocence. No one believed him. Story goes that no one will ever forget the sight of his terrified eyes as he crashed down into the darkness, or the sound of his scream as it echoed into that black hole.'

'And was he innocent?' I expected him to tell me that a few days later the real truth had come out. Poor Dobie was an innocent man. But he didn't. He only shrugged. 'No more children went missing after that . . .' Then he added ominously. 'Not here anyway.'

'What do you mean by that?'

'Wouldn't that be a perfect crime? You kill, someone else gets the blame and then you move on somewhere else and kill again. Who's going to suspect? The crime in the last town has been solved. Case closed.'

I wanted to say he should be writing murder mysteries, but at that second I began to shake so badly it scared me. My teeth, my bones, my whole body. Couldn't stop. I was freezing with cold, yet I felt as if I was on fire.

He touched my brow. 'You're burning up, son.'

I tried to tell him I would be fine in a minute, just needed a minute, but the words wouldn't come. I couldn't stop shaking.

And I knew it was a lie. I wasn't going to be fine.

'Maybe I should take you to a doctor.'

Couldn't have him do that. A doctor might mean hospital and questions and the Dark Man finding me again.

I gripped at his sleeve. Managed one word. 'NO.'

I was trying to think, and I was too ill to think. Didn't know what to say. I had no choice, or if I did, I couldn't find it. I decided to go with a lie I had been living with to protect myself. 'Home. My granny.' I pointed to the town, unseen over the hill. Maybe he would be on his way now, let me go mine.

'Your granny?'

'Bella Bartell,' I mumbled.

Suddenly, he was laughing so hard I thought he would split his trousers. 'Bella's your granny?'

He knew her! That was all I needed.

'Never told me she had family. Well, you learn something new every day.' He pulled me to my feet. I tried to stand but my jelly legs just wouldn't hold me up. All of a sudden he had me in his arms, carrying me. I couldn't protest. I felt as if I was slipping into my own black hole.

He laughed. 'I've saved the life of Bella Bartell's grandson. This must deserve a feed.'

'Who are you?' My voice trembled and sounded a million miles away.

He took a long time to answer that one. And his answer was the last thing I heard before I dropped into unconsciousness. 'They call me Catman.'

10

Ryan couldn't believe what he was seeing. He moved further into the shade of the trees and watched in amazement. Ramon was being carried over the field by the most evil man he had ever known. Catman.

The whole town, every child in it, knew about him. Everyone was petrified by the legend of him. He came and went in the night, they said, stealing children. Now he had Ramon. Ramon was unconscious. Maybe even dead. His head lolled back, his arm hung limp. He wanted to run forward and snatch Ramon out of his grasp. But maybe, just maybe, Catman would snatch Ryan instead.

He watched Catman, fascinated, as he strode through the bushes. The wild hair, the hard face, a mouth that seemed to be set in a permanent snarl. He looked evil. Ryan realised he was holding his breath. At last he drew his eyes away from Catman, looked back at the limp figure in Catman's arms. What had he done to Ramon?

He was heading in the direction of Bella Bartell's house. Bella Bartell and Catman. In Ryan's mind they went together like Alien and Predator, one as bad as the other. It was here, to Bella's house, that Catman always came. She was the only person who would tolerate him. No wonder Ryan didn't trust Bella. Something very sinister was going on. Ryan had a hunch about it. And good detectives always followed their hunches.

Did he really believe that Ramon was Bella's grandson? He had always thought she had no family, and suddenly she plucks a grandson out of nowhere. No, truth to tell, he didn't. Now this evil man was back. At school, he had heard others telling tales of Catman: that he had the strength of ten men. Superhuman strength. Inhuman strength. Ryan stepped back into the trees as Catman's eyes jerked towards him – as if he'd caught sight of his movements. He put his hand over his mouth to stop himself from breathing, in case that inhuman hearing of his could catch the sound of his softest breath. Ryan was afraid of even looking at the man. He had heard so many stories about him, of all the evil things he had done. Stories that said if you looked dead into his eyes you could be turned to stone.

He watched as Catman reached Bella's house, kicked at the door with his foot to open it, and disappeared inside.

Now he had even more to investigate. Things had certainly hotted up since Ramon had come into his life. But he couldn't leave Ramon in there and not do anything. He had to make sure that Ramon was safe.

Bella watched from the window. Couldn't believe either what she was seeing. Catman and the boy. How had they got together? What had happened to the boy? What had brought Catman back here? Hadn't she told him he was in danger in this town? People were going missing. Why would he never listen? Here he was back, and this time she couldn't be responsible for his safety.

It was their bickering that dragged me back to consciousness. Catman still had me in his arms, hadn't had time to lay me down anywhere before she was berating him. As soon as he stepped over her threshold she was at him. They greeted each other like long-lost enemies. 'I told you never to come back here! You're not welcome here! Do you never listen?'

'Shut up, old woman! I'm a free man. I can do as I please. Now clear those cats from the couch so I can put the boy down.'

She shooed Mata and Hari from their places and Catman laid me down gently. 'And what are you doing with this boy anyway?' she asked.

'Saving his life if you want to know.'

I put a shaky hand up to explain. She pushed my hand down. 'He doesn't need the likes of you to save his life.'

'Well, actually . . .' I wanted to tell her what had happened, but I was brushed aside.

'He would have gone down Dobie's Doom if I hadn't grabbed him,' Catman said.

That shut her up. She bent down to me. 'So you went back there, did you?'

'What do you mean, "back there"?' Catman didn't wait for me to answer. 'He was standing up for that daft gowk, Lenny. He was being tormented by a bunch of

47

boys. Superman here decided to help him, so they turned on him.'

I wanted to answer that but I hadn't the strength.

'That's where I found him last night. Up in the valley,' Bella said. 'He saw something up there, but he hasn't said what . . .'

Catman laughed. 'Ha! Would that be a flying saucer? Or maybe little green men?'

Bella wasn't laughing. 'Well, he saw something that frightened him anyway.' She looked at me. 'That's why you went back there, isn't it?'

She was right. It was. I had been drawn there. I wanted to see the place in daylight, see if it held any menace now.

'So where did this story about him being your long-lost grandson come from? Who's going to believe that?'

Bella looked at me again and tutted. 'Couldn't you have kept your mouth shut?'

Then she turned back to Catman. 'The boy's a run-away. Can't remember a thing, so he tells me. Doesn't want to be turned in. I needed a cover story for Dr Mulvey. You can understand that, can't you? You're a runaway yourself, Catman.'

And then Catman wasn't laughing. His face suddenly grew serious. He looked from Bella to me. 'On the run, eh? Know the feeling, son. Your secret's safe with me.'

Bella gave him a shove. 'Blinking well better be or I'll make you sorry.'

Catman pulled a chair over and straddled it. 'So, is saving your grandson's life worth a meal or not?'

I couldn't understand why he was so eager to sample

Bella's cooking. I thought I would eat anything, but I drew the line at what she cooked up. I watched her ladle something brown and gooey on to a plate. Catman wasn't so fussy. I watched in horror as he wolfed it down as if it was a gourmet meal. 'You're a grand cook, Bella,' he said. 'Don't know why some lucky man never snapped you up.'

I would have thought you only had to look at her face to know that.

Catman came up to my room when I was safely tucked up in bed with Mata and Hari close beside me. He loomed above me. Bits of brown mush were caught in his beard. I wanted desperately to sleep. Had to ask him.

'You're a runaway too? Why did you run away?'

There was a pause. 'That's my secret,' he said.

Secrets, I thought, I was finding them everywhere. Catman had one and so had I. And I wondered again . . . what was Bella's?

11

Something pulled me from sleep. I half opened my eyes, lay listening. It was dark. I was sweating – only wanted to sleep, get back to my for once dreamless sleep. At first I thought it was the constant rain stabbing at my window that had woken me up. Then perhaps it was either Mata or Hari trying to scratch their way in. But when I moved, there they were, one of them tucked close to my chest, the other lying by my head. Finally, I realised what the sound was. Pebbles were being thrown at the window, scattering against the glass.

I got up. My legs were still like jelly. I held on to the dresser and stumbled to the window. At first I could see nothing. Here at the back of the house I was only looking on to Bella's jungle of a garden, and beyond that to the wood and the dark hills. Then I saw a movement. A face. It was Ryan's face staring up at me. He was hiding in the bushes, trying to look as if he wasn't there. When he spotted me at the window he leapt out and began waving madly at me. It was almost funny.

'Come on down,' he mouthed.

I shook my head at first. I wanted to go back to bed. My pyjamas clung to me with sweat. I tried to mouth to him that I wasn't well, but Ryan kept beckoning me like mad, and I knew if I didn't go down and see him there was a chance he would stay there till morning. Finally, I nodded, pointed down towards the back door.

It was night. I crept as silently as I could down the stairs. I could hear the whispering voices of Catman and Bella in the living room. He was still here. I tiptoed past the door, pulled on an old raincoat of Bella's with a hood and slipped my bare feet into a pair of her wellies. I pushed the kitchen door open and stepped out into the back yard. At first I couldn't see Ryan at all. Then he appeared from amongst the trees with what looked like a bush on his head. I might have laughed until I realised he couldn't look any dafter than me wearing Bella's raincoat and her wellies.

'Camouflage,' he explained, pointing at his head. He pulled me into the shrubbery and out of sight.

'Why all the secrecy?' I asked.

'Because you obviously don't know what you're in amongst, Ramon. Catman is a dangerous man. They're dangerous people.' He nodded to where Catman and Bella sat in the living room. I imagined them drinking tea from Bella's teapot shaped like a cat. Didn't seem life threatening to me at all. But what was Ryan imagining?

He touched my hand and must have felt how hot it was. 'What have they done to you?'

'I've got a fever, Ryan. Nothing mysterious. Bella . . . my gran isn't dangerous. Neither is Catman.'

'Catman's dangerous all right.'

'You know Catman?'

He began to whisper breathlessly. 'Everybody knows

51

Catman. He's like one of those urban legends. He turns up here in the town now and then. Bella Bartell is the only one who'll give him house room.'

'She takes in strays, you know that.'

'Everyone knows stories about him. The most evil man who ever lived.'

I thought about that, tried to remember stories I had heard in my short memory. The most evil man who ever lived? 'Would that not be that Hitler guy?'

Ryan shook that away as if I'd said something really stupid. 'No, Catman is really evil. He lives in a dark world. He bites the head off rats and sucks their blood.'

Now I did laugh and Ryan didn't like it. 'It's not funny, Ramon. Have you seen his teeth? Brown, stained with the blood of dead rats.'

'Oh, come on, Ryan. He bites the heads off rats and sucks their blood? He just eats normal things like everyone else.' Then I remembered Bella's goo and wondered if that was true.

'He comes and goes,' Ryan went on. 'And when he comes that's when the strange things happen. My budgie died the last time he was here. 'I almost laughed again at that, till I saw he was deadly serious. 'And people go missing.'

'Do you know any of these people who go missing?' I asked him.

'No, not exactly. I just hear about them. Nobody ever believes me. My dad says people move on in this town. They get other jobs; no one stays here long or makes real friends. That's what my dad says.' He kicked at the ground. 'Nobody ever listens.'

I could understand that feeling. So could Bella. No one ever listened to her either. 'Catman saved my life, Ryan.' I said it and regretted it right away. I hadn't wanted to tell anyone about where I'd been or what my suspicions were. 'I mean, I was up at that Dobie's Doom and there was this gang of boys, they were tormenting –'

'Let me guess,' he interrupted. 'Daft Lenny?' He laughed. 'Everybody does that.' He said it as if it didn't matter.

'They were threatening to drop him down that waterfall. And then they were screaming at him. He's terrified of anybody screaming.'

Ryan only laughed. 'I know. He says that's how the aliens talk. They scream at each other.'

'It's not funny, Ryan. He could have fallen down that Dobie's Doom'

'Lenny's daft,' Ryan said. 'Everybody picks on him.'

'But you wouldn't?'

He stared at me, as if he was trying to figure out the answer I wanted to hear. He looked so serious, yet he still had a bush tied to his head. I really had to force myself not to laugh. 'You would have helped him too, wouldn't you?' I asked him.

'Well, I suppose . . . of course I would,' he finished with decision. 'I'm so glad you didn't go down Dobie's Doom, Ramon.'

'Does everybody know about that place?'

He nodded. 'Lots of people are supposed to have fallen down there. Some fell and some, they say . . . didn't actually go of their own free will.' His voice became quiet and mysterious. Ryan seemed to be enjoying telling me the stories. 'Men have got rid of rich wives down there, so they say. Once the body's gone there's no proof of murder. No proof. It's called Habeas Corpus. You have to have a body to prove the crime.'

And for the first time I thought maybe that was where the missing people had gone. Thrown down Dobie's Doom for some reason. I could picture it all, remembering the terror I had felt as I clung on to that wet grass. Clinging for my life, saved in the nick of time. 'Well, it was your Catman who saved me,' I told him. 'Hardly the thing for the most evil man in the world to be doing, eh?'

Ryan had an immediate answer for that. 'He saved you for a reason. He wants you for something else.'

Nothing was going to convince Ryan. He wanted a mystery. He wanted a villain. And Catman seemed the perfect bad guy.

'My dad could help you . . . if you need help . . .'

I certainly didn't want Ryan telling his dad I needed help. I thought it might be time to remind him I was supposed to be Bella's grandson. 'Honest, Ryan, I know my granny is a bit eccentric, but she's OK. She's kind-hearted. She loves taking in strays. She's giving this Catman a meal to thank him for helping me. And then he'll be on his way. OK?'

He didn't look happy about that at all. 'I just want you to know . . . I'm here for you. Run to my house if you need me. If you have to wake me in the middle of the night, you'll know my window. I have a nightlight on the ledge, a model of a spaceship.'

He nodded his head and his bush fell half over his eye.

I tried not to laugh. That would have been cruel. Because I knew Ryan meant every word.

The two boys were being watched from a distance. The Reaper, hidden from view. One of them, the boy Ryan, was nosy, always had been. But the other, this new boy, his curiosity was dangerous. Why did he think this boy was going to cause trouble for him? He was a boy who wouldn't let things go once he started to become suspicious. Like a dog with a bone. Maybe the Reaper could use him; let him join his little band. After all, he didn't have a boy in his collection . . . yet. Maybe he shouldn't be thinking of getting rid of him after all.

Catman was gone when I crept back into the house. Must have gone out by the front door. Bella was in a bad mood. I heard her muttering, 'He should never have come back. Too dangerous.'

Was she mad? Everyone else seemed to think so. What was dangerous for Catman? The most evil man in the world, Ryan thought. A man with a secret. But if it hadn't been for Catman, I reminded myself as I drifted off to sleep again, I wouldn't have been lying there in a warm bed with Mata's tail dangling over my face and Hari curled up on my chest. I would have hurtled down that dark, deep well of water, going where? To hell, Catman had said. The thought made me sweat and shake, and Hari trembled a little at my movement.

Strange history about that valley. Witches and aliens

and innocent men sent tumbling, screaming to their deaths . . . some maybe not so innocent. No wonder it excited Ryan.

I could understand that. There was a mystery up in that valley. There was a mystery here in this town. And it intrigued me. I knew it was stupid; I should just want to move on. But a big part of me wanted to find out what that mystery was.

12

I was walking down a long corridor, fire on every side of me, looking for a way out. But how? There was no escape. I was going the wrong way. It was as if I was watching myself in a film. I wanted to yell out, 'Go back. You're moving straight towards the fire!' But when I opened my mouth all that came out was a high-pitched whine. I was looking for someone, knew they were close by. I wanted to call out their name, but I couldn't remember who it was I was searching for.

Then I saw a dark shadow in the fire, blacking out the flames. Someone come to rescue me. I reached out towards them, but then I knew it wasn't who I thought it was. No saviour. It was someone else. Someone scary.

It was the Dark Man.

I wanted to go back, but I couldn't move. My feet were glued to the ground. He was reaching for me, his big hands, strange misshapen hands like spades, reaching out for me. He had me at last. This time there was no escape.

I began to shake. The shadow came closer. His hands gripped me. His face came close to mine, his eyes the eyes of a madman. Why couldn't I scream?

And suddenly it wasn't the Dark Man at all. The face changed, became horrible. Became a monster. A monster with a face like a zombie. I began to struggle to get away. I was surrounded by madness. The hands were shaking me, the face began to laugh. The fire was all around me.

Now I did begin to scream. Scream and struggle to be free. And the monster let me go. He clamped his hands over his ears and I stumbled back, still screaming.

And the monster was afraid.

'Lenny! Lenny! Let him be!'

It was Bella's voice I heard. I opened my eyes, and she had me by the arm, holding me up. I was coming out of a nightmare.

I was in her living room. How had I got here? Bella caught me. 'Shut up,' she said, shaking me. 'You're frightening the life out of Lenny.'

I blinked and looked at the monster. Not a monster at all. It was Lenny. He looked terrified, filling the doorway with the bulk of him.

Bella snapped at him, 'Come on, give me a hand here.' And the monster with the spades for hands wrapped them round me and carried me and set me down on Bella's settee.

I looked back at his big face. Round, with red cheeks and a nose like a tomato. Nothing to be afraid of, I thought. The monster was Lenny. And I was ashamed. Ashamed because I had been afraid just because he was different.

'How did you get down these stairs?' Bella answered the question herself. 'You must have been sleepwalking.'

Lenny stood behind her, peering over her shoulder. Bella put a wrinkled hand on my brow. 'You're burning up again.'

She went off for a cold cloth. Lenny still stood there, staring down at me. I wanted to say I was sorry, but hadn't the strength to speak.

'Did they get you?' His voice was a surprise. It was a man's voice, low and gruff.

I just looked at him. What was he talking about? He moved a fraction closer, whispered, 'Did they come for you?'

At first I thought he meant the boys who had been tormenting him. Then I realised he was talking about aliens. I tried to say there were no aliens, but Lenny was getting excited now. 'They'll come back. They always come back. They've got their eye on you.'

Did he say it to frighten me? He wasn't the type who could frighten anyone. Maybe at first, with his appearance, but not for long. There was an innocence in that big face of his. But his voice was different, low and filled with menace.

'They'll come back for me. And I'll help them. They won't hurt me this time. They promised.'

He began to grin. A wide vacant grin that shouldn't have scared me, but it did. 'I'm important to them,' he said. 'But they're coming for you.'

The way he said it sent a cold shiver down my back.

I was glad Bella came back in then. 'Lenny!' she snapped at him. 'Don't talk your nonsense here. Get in the kitchen. I'll give you something to eat.' Lenny shuffled into her kitchen, but just for a second he turned back and looked at Bella. I saw his dark look behind her back. As if he hated her. Had I imagined it? A moment later he was gone, and I couldn't be sure. Bella slapped the cold, damp cloth on my forehead. Not much of a gentle touch, I thought, but it made me feel better. 'I've called Dr Mulvey,' she said. 'He's coming back.'

She hummed softly as she waited for him to arrive. I noticed then her computer was switched on. She saw me looking at it. 'I was looking for you, to be honest,' she said. 'Looking for signs of a missing boy.'

She didn't have to tell me there were none. No one was looking for me. No one missed me.

'It's strange you're not on any missing person register,' she said.

She was waiting for me to tell her something about myself, but how could I begin? I had no beginning.

'When you're feeling better you can have a look yourself,' she said finally.

She went upstairs and left me. The computer lay there on the desk as if it was waiting for me, urging me towards it. I couldn't resist it. I stumbled to her desk, sat on her soft leather chair. Only I wasn't going to look for a missing boy.

I was going to look for a dead one.

I wanted to find out if there were any reports about a boy, recently dead, or a boy's body as yet unidentified, but one that my family assumed was me. It was the only explanation, surely?

I would look in the recent news. Maybe I had been involved in a major train crash and had stumbled off into the night, not knowing who I was. Everyone thought I was dead. Couldn't that be the case?

I brought up a news website, one that Bella had been looking at, and looked through the archives of news stories over the last year.

Airplane crashes, train crashes, motorway pile-ups, death and destruction.

Bombings.

Innocents dying.

No wonder Catman had sounded so despairing.

The big story, of course, was this London bombing. There were newspaper reports about it everywhere. And for the first time I saw a photograph of the bomber himself. He looked hard, staring severely at the camera. I found myself staring back at him. Why had he done such a terrible thing? It had been sheer luck, they said, that no one else had been hurt or killed. No luck for him, however. He had been blown to bits along with his bomb. It had gone off too early.

The lone bomber, they called him. Faisal had talked about him, said his dad was sure he was part of a conspiracy. Could that be true? Were there more like him around? I shuddered at the thought of it, scrolled away from the story, and his photo. It made me shiver.

But I was looking for my own story. I was looking for me. Still I could find nothing. Neither missing nor dead. No bodies of boys as yet unidentified.

So why was no one looking for me?

Why didn't I have a mother or a father out there, desperately searching for me, asking questions, hounding the press?

Because they thought I was dead already?

What was I? Who was I?

I began to feel as hopeless as Catman.

I was back on the settee when I heard Dr Mulvey come in the front door, unannounced. I was almost in tears. No one, it seemed, cared about me. Something of my feelings must have shown in my face.

'What's happened to you this time? You look awful.'

I didn't have to answer. Bella was bustling back downstairs and was good at answering for me. 'He decided to go exploring, even though I told him to stay near the cottage. Off he went in all that rain! Almost fell into Dobie's Doom.'

Dr Mulvey shook his head. 'Oh, never to be seen again. It goes deep down into the ground – nobody knows how deep.'

'He's heard some of the stories,' Bella said.

'Really cheered me up,' I mumbled.

'It turned this place into a town nobody really lives in,' Bella said. 'People began to think it was an unlucky place. What do you call a town like that?'

'A ghost town,' I said, but nobody listened.

She went on as if I might be interested. 'It's only recently with the airport expanding and the big computer place opening up that people have started living here again. New houses springing up all over the place. But only houses. There are no shops, no church, no heart to it. There's a name for a town like that too.'

'I think they call it a sleeper town,' the doctor said.

'No,' Bella said. 'A dormitory town, that's what you call it. A dormitory town.'

Dr Mulvey examined me again. I was waiting for him

to tell me I was about to die. I had only hours left. I was sure of it. That was how bad I felt. But all he said was, 'Constitution of an ox, this boy. Soon be on the mend. Just needs a few more days' rest and he'll be fighting fit again. But just to be on the safe side I'll pop in first thing in the morning.'

Bella helped me back up to the bedroom. I think she was getting ready to charm the doctor with her feminine wiles.

But I was glad to be going back to bed. I was feeling down, sick, sore and hopeless. If only I could sleep, but my mind was too full for sleep. I lay in bed with Mata and Hari curled tight against me. They seemed to have taken to me, and at that moment I felt they were the only living things that cared about me. I couldn't sleep, not properly. I'd close my eyes and once again I would be back on that computer, desperately searching for some hint of who I was, and finding nothing. I was nobody. And all I could see was the photo of that London bomber, and he was suddenly laughing at me, shouting at me to 'Run!'

13

WEDNESDAY

Ryan was on his way to school when he saw Dr Mulvey's car draw up outside Bella Bartell's house. He got out, walked up the path and rapped on the door. Ryan slipped behind the trees and watched. He pulled out his notebook. The doctor was back again. Why? Was Ramon any worse? Maybe the doctor and Bella were in it together, drugging him up for their own evil intentions. He'd always thought there was something funny about the doctor as well.

If only he didn't have to go to school. Why were his parents so sure going to school was the right thing to do? He could learn so much more watching things, studying people, listening.

It was Bella who opened the door to the doctor, smiling at him as if she was seventeen. Ryan waited till the door was closed before pushing open the gate, wishing it didn't creak the way it did, and tiptoeing up the path to the side window. It was open. Bella Bartell's windows were always open to let her cats in and out. He could hear Bella talking to the doctor, listened carefully.

'He must stay with me for a few more days, doctor. He's not well enough to be moved.'

The doctor was wiping his glasses with his handkerchief. 'I could have him looked at in hospital if you're really worried about him.'

Bella cut in sharply. 'No. Don't want him in the hospital. He'll be fine here with his granny.'

Forcing him to stay, Ryan was thinking as he moved away from the window. He was sure of it. Bella Bartell had her own evil reasons for keeping Ramon there, grandson or not.

Ryan turned away from the window and yelled. There, right in front of him, his darkest nightmare.

Catman!

His hair was every bit as wild as he had imagined. His teeth, what he had of them, stained brown, from all that rats' blood he drank. Catman let out a low growl like a wild beast, as he reached out a grimy hand and grabbed at him. No way was Catman getting a hold of him! Ryan darted out from under his grasp, gave him a push and sent him stumbling backwards, then he jumped to the side and ran. He had never run so fast, flying down the path and almost leaping over the gate. He glanced back once and Catman was nowhere to be seen. He was shaking with fear, sure he was suddenly going to materialise right in front of him, envelope him in his coat, make him disappear too.

He could hardly get his breath but he didn't stop running. He ran all the way to school. And all he could think about was that Ramon was in that house, with Bella Bartell and Catman. That couldn't be safe for him.

He needed Ryan's help badly.

'You quite happy to stay with your gran for a few days more?' The doctor asked. He had come up to see me before he left. I glanced at Bella. Bella was there, hovering by my bed like some ancient crone, as if she really was my anxious grandmother.

She was worried about me, the old dear. Bringing the doctor back in to see me showed just how concerned she really was. And wasn't that something I missed? Someone caring about me?

I nodded at the doctor, and he left with Bella close behind him, giggling like a schoolgirl.

I must have fallen asleep again, but when I woke it was still raining; another grey day with rain battering against the window. I could hear voices, Bella's and someone else's in the kitchen. Something made me get up and tread softly to the door.

It was Catman she was talking to, whispering softly as if she didn't want anyone, especially someone in the house, to hear her words.

'There's someone else gone missing now. The girl who used to work in the charity shop isn't there any more. And still no one's suspicious!' Bella sounded angry.

Catman was dismissing that. 'A girl who only came here a few weeks ago and took a temporary job at the charity shop?' he said. 'And now she's gone? Perhaps

66

she's got a new job in London. No one else thinks she's gone missing, only you. You should forget about all this. You're becoming obsessed.'

'It's always the same thing. The perfect person goes missing: the one nobody is going to miss!'

She was right, I thought, like Catman's story of the perfect murder. This was the perfect abduction. No one to miss you, no one to care.

I would be the perfect case too, except to everyone I was now Bella's grandson, and she would miss me. Maybe, for once, I had landed lucky.

'You're in danger every time you come here.' Bella said it as if she was genuinely worried about Catman. 'The boy's in danger too. Why does nobody listen to me?'

And Catman's dark, depressed voice answered her.

'They can take me any time. I really couldn't care less.'

14

The Dark Man had lost track of the boy. He hated to admit it, but he had no notion now of where the boy had gone. He had only been hours behind him and the boy had slipped into the shadows once again. He tried to tell himself it didn't matter. Not now. Now was too late. The boy hadn't remembered. Even if he did, at this late stage, the knowledge would mean nothing to him. But what else did he know? That was what they had to find out.

He would continue his search. It wasn't in him to give up on anything. Another few days and it wouldn't matter.

So he would scroll news reports, use all his resources to track him down; he had found him before. If luck was with him, he could find him again.

This time he wouldn't lose him.

I dreamt of the Dark Man again. Weird dreams of him being with me, helping me. In my dream I was smiling at him. Laughing. He had some sort of pole in his hand. At first, in the dream, I thought it was a fishing rod. He was teaching me to fish.

Then the rod turned into something sinister. A rifle. He was showing me how to use a gun. I reached out to take the gun from him and, suddenly, it was pointing straight at me. He was aiming it at my face, his smile changing to a terrifying grimace. I tried to step away from him, but he was reaching for me, and no matter how far from him I moved, his arms, like elastic, grew ever longer, reaching out for me, sinuous as a snake, weaving their way towards me. I couldn't breathe, began to shake, calling for someone, realising even in the dream that I couldn't remember who to call for.

I rolled around in the bed. I felt the cats leap away from me in panic. I could feel sweat pouring from me. I prayed, *Please let it be a nightmare*, for I could still see those rubbery arms winding their way through the window, through the door.

I tried to force myself awake. Had to make sure this was only a dream.

Yet, had it been a dream? Maybe, I thought – and the thought only made me shake all the more – maybe it was a memory. Because it wasn't the first time I had seen myself laugh with the Dark Man. Why? Who was he? And the terrifying thought came to me again, not for the first time . . . was he my father?

Bella was holding me when I opened my eyes. 'Are you OK? You had a bad dream.'

I didn't want to sleep any more, didn't want the Dark Man invading my dreams again. I tried to sit up and Bella fluffed up the pillows behind me. How long had she been sitting beside my bed? I wondered.

'Who is this Dark Man? You say his name over and over. You're so afraid of him.'

'Just a dream,' I muttered.

Bella shook her head. 'Your life seems to be full of bad dreams.'

What could I say? Tell her all about the Dark Man? I wanted to, but . . . what would be the point? What could she do?

No one ever listened to her, she was fond of telling me.

'Who is this Dark Man?' she asked again.

'He wants to kill me, Bella,' I said. 'I don't know why. I know something, can't remember what. First he wants to find out what that something is . . . then he'll kill me.'

I couldn't tell if she believed me. Or if she thought the fever was making me hallucinate. She touched my hand gently. 'You're safe here. I'll keep the Dark Man away.'

Ryan couldn't eat a thing. He wanted someone to confide in too. But his dad, his mum, they would never understand. Every time he thought of Ramon in that house with Catman his blood ran cold. Ramon was in danger. Ryan just knew it. How could he help him?

'I made your favourite, Ryan,' his mother told him as if he didn't know. Spaghetti bolognese, heaps of it, and he couldn't face it at all.

Since Ramon had come here there had been nothing but excitement. Catman was back. Someone else had gone missing. And the days had suddenly become dark and miserable. All since Ramon had arrived in town.

He'd heard his dad used a word for that. Catalyst. Ramon was the catalyst for all these things.

'What is wrong with you, Ryan?'

He decided to tell them a half truth. 'It's that Catman . . . He's back.'

His mother tutted. 'He's just an old tramp.'

'He's not, Mum, he's . . .' He wanted to tell them about the biting off rats' heads thing, but it was too gross for his mother; she would probably puke. 'He's dangerous,' was all he said.

His dad, to his surprise, agreed with him. 'I don't think he should be allowed to wander about the town the way he does. Adults aren't around by day . . . mostly working, and there are vulnerable children here. Maybe Ryan's right.' He looked at Ryan and smiled. 'You keep well back from him, promise?'

'Of course I will, Dad.' He took a deep breath. 'But you know what that Bella Bartell's like. She takes in all the strays and he's one of them. I see him going into that Bella's . . . Do you think that her grandson's in any danger?'

'Bella Bartell is a bad-tempered, grumpy old woman, Ryan,' his mother said. 'But surely even she would look after her grandson.'

Maybe his mum was right, but he intended to keep a close eye on the house. Protect Ramon. Maybe if being a halfwit ran in the family, Ramon might be as daft as his gran. He would need somebody sensible like Ryan to look after him.

15

The girl saw the cell door slide open. A shaft of green light seeped into her prison. For the first time she saw how small the room she had been kept in was. Square, with dark metal walls, a camp bed for her to sleep on, a bucket in the corner.

She stood against the wall, too afraid to move. She waited. Was someone, or something, about to appear in that strange green light? She imagined a dark shadow, huge and menacing, blocking the doorway, and she backed further against the wall, half hoping the wall would swallow her up, that she could melt into the steel, find herself in another room, another world. Free. She had dreamt of nothing else since she had been brought here. When? How long had she been here? In the darkness, there was no day and no night. Nothing, but terror.

Still she waited, breathlessly, and she watched. But nothing came.

There was a strange silence. She took a step forward. Then another. Was this freedom at last?

At the doorway she hesitated again. Her heart was bursting with fear at the thought of stepping outside this cell. Was this a trick? She remembered the faces she had seen. Blank, inhuman, staring down at her. Had she fainted? She must have, for she could remember nothing after that, but waking up in the dark.

She almost stepped back inside the cell at the memory of those faces.

But the call of freedom was too strong. She peered round the doorway, blinking in the eerie green light, saw down a long corridor. Was she alone here? She wanted to call out, but it had been so long since she'd used her voice she wondered if she could still make a sound.

And what if she wasn't alone? What if her call alerted her captor and he came and she was pushed in that cell again?

Which way to go? To the left? To the right? Which way lay freedom and escape? Escape from where? Where was she? And was there any way out?

She stepped into the corridor. One step. She hesitated, listened again, heard nothing. She began to walk faster. She was going to be free! And anywhere was better than being trapped in that cell.

She caught her breath. What was that sound? Echoes? She stopped, listened. A sound coming from somewhere ahead of her, beyond the corner, far into the darkness at the end of the long corridor. A sound she couldn't understand. The girl held her breath, waited, afraid to move, afraid to take a step back or a step forward. What was that sound?

And then *they* appeared, bathed in the green light, glowing green themselves. They came from the darkness, and she found her voice at last in a long, terrified scream. She saw what was making that sound and her screams bounced off the walls. It couldn't be real what she was seeing. She turned and began to run back the way she'd come, still screaming, hearing them behind her, faster, closing in on her. She saw her cell door, still open. But beginning to close slowly! Nowhere else to go. She ran inside, leapt on to the bed, prayed the door would shut tight before they reached it. Here they came and still she screamed, and the door was closing too slowly!

'Close!' she screamed. 'Don't let them come inside!'

The Reaper smiled. He slammed the cell door shut. The girl was safely trapped once more. He had it timed to perfection. It was good, he had decided long ago, to give them a little taste of freedom. And then let them see what lay outside their cells.

Waiting. Watching. Guarding.

And once they saw . . . he knew they would never try to escape again.

16

It was time for another. The Reaper needed more. No wonder he thought they were all fools. The clues were all there for anyone to spot. Yet so far there had not been the least suspicion that anything was going on. Apart from the old woman, and no one listened to her. How easy it was to fool people.

Perhaps the boy should be the next, the Reaper thought. No. He decided that the boy could wait. His time would come. Perhaps he would leave the best till last. There was nowhere for the boy to go now. He would get him when he moved on, and how easy would that be? Another one not missed.

For the moment, it would be a treat to keep him guessing. So who should it be? The Reaper watched the street, empty by day, people off at work, children at school. A town where no one really knew their neighbour. A town where no one was missed. Perfect.

And then he saw the one. The one who would be next.

He came out of the bushes, his long dark coat trailing on the ground. He was heading for the old woman's house. He was chewing something, had bits of it caught in his grey beard. Another one who would never be missed.

The Reaper smiled. The one the children called Catman: he would be his next specimen.

The sweat was pouring out of me, caught in another nightmare. People running and shouting. Chaos all around me. I was too hot. But I couldn't stop running. I had to get somewhere fast. I had something important – no, more than important – to tell someone. Something even more important to find. I knew a secret. It seemed in my dream the secret was behind a door and I was heading for the door. It was opening slowly as I headed for it. A door set into a dark sky, and the secret was hidden behind that door. I had been behind the door before, knew its secrets. If I could get through the door again, I would know everything. Yet the more I ran, the further away the door seemed to be. I was never getting any closer. Time was running out. I began to yell, scream. I had to make it in time. I had to.

'Son, son, what's wrong?' It was Catman, shaking me out of the nightmare. I pushed him away, closed my eyes, tried to recapture the picture of that door. But it was gone. The door had closed.

Catman gripped me by the shoulders. 'You were having a bad dream. It's the fever,' he said. 'I'll get a damp cloth to cool you down.' He got up to leave.

'I can't be here. I have to go.' I tried to step out of the bed, sat up and the room seemed to spin as if I was on a rollercoaster. I fell back on to the pillows.

'You're going nowhere,' he said.

'Have to.' I said that over and over. 'Have to.'

'Why?' he asked, sitting himself back down on the bed next to me. 'What's so urgent you have to go now?'

I shook my head. Couldn't answer that. I could remember nothing.

'I have to save somebody,' was all I said.

'Let them save themselves,' Catman said.

'But I can't do that. Someone's relying on me. I'm sure they are.'

'You were shouting about "the Dark Man" . . . "Don't let him get me."' He watched me closely. 'Who is this Dark Man?'

'Someone who's after me . . . I've managed to stay a step ahead of him, but I'm always scared he'll find me again. He's after me because of what I know.'

'Go to the police. Tell them.'

'Can't. I don't know who to trust. I don't know who I am.'

'You're right about not trusting anyone. People always let you down. Too much evil in the world.'

And I knew in that moment I didn't agree with that. 'No. There's more good than evil.' Hadn't I seen it with the people who had helped me? 'More good than bad,' I said. 'It's a wonderful world, Catman. I'm only just discovering it. Since I woke up in that stairwell, I've found out so many wonderful things. Men landed on the moon. We beat the Nazis. Good people always win.'

Where did all that sadness in his eyes come from? 'Wait till you're older,' he said. 'You'll soon learn. The world's hell-bent on self-destruction. And we all deserve it. Look after number one. That's the philosophy to live by.'

'You're forgetting you saved my life.'

He shrugged. 'And what did I risk? Nothing. I scared off a bunch of bully teenagers. Would I have saved you if it meant risking my own life?' He shook his head. 'I'm afraid not, son. I'm just not a hero.'

What had happened to Catman to make him so bitter?

What would a good detective do? Ryan was wondering. He hadn't seen Ramon today, and he had to know how he was. He had visions of him being bound up in Bella's cellar, force-fed rat droppings, being turned into a disciple of Catman.

Maybe Bella knew nothing about it . . . Then he dismissed that idea. She must know; all that dottiness was an act, he was convinced of that.

He stood at the gate at the bottom of her garden and watched the house. He was half waiting for some kind of distress signal from Ramon. But nothing came.

He thought he might just go up to the front door and ask about him. But in his imagination Bella dragged him inside and that was the last ever seen of him. He hadn't told anyone he was coming here. How could he tell his mum and dad? They had warned him to stay away. They would go spare if they knew he'd come back. And his friends at school? Truth was, he didn't have many friends at school. And the ones he had he wasn't close to. Certainly not close enough to confide in. Anyway, this was his case. He was going to solve it.

If he could only leave some clue about where he was going, something that would keep him safe, and it came to him. His mobile phone. He would email his computer from his mobile phone.

If I have not returned by six o'clock you will find me trapped in Bella Bartell's house.

There, he'd done it. Now he felt safe. What did they call it in crime movies? . . . His insurance. That was Ryan's insurance that he would be safe in Bella's house.

He opened the gate and walked up the path to the front door.

17

It was Bella Bartell who opened the door to him. Ryan stood back, expecting her to lunge forward and attack him. She ran her fingers through her tousled hair and licked her lips. *Disgusting woman*, he thought.

'What do you want?' One of the cats appeared, the one with the wicked eye. It entwined itself round her legs.

Ryan swallowed. 'I was . . .' He stopped, his throat too dry to go on. 'How's your grandson?' He got it out after an age.

'My Ramon?' she said. 'He's got a cold, but he'll be fine, thank you very much.'

Now was his boldest moment. 'Can I come in and see him?'

She seemed to think about it. Was she thinking that here was another victim? Was he mad even taking the risk of going inside her house? He half hoped she would refuse him entry. Yet, when she did – 'He's sleeping,' she said. 'Sleep's the best thing for him' – he found himself even more suspicious. Refused entry. It would go down in his notebook.

She began closing the door. 'I'll tell him you were here.'

He wanted to shove his foot inside, keep the door open. He wanted to be old enough, strong enough to take matters into his own hands and check for himself. Ramon was in there, and so was Bella Bartell, and even worse, Catman.

She held the door slightly ajar, peered round. 'You can go away now,' she said. Then she closed it in his face.

He stood for only a moment. He could do nothing, not by himself. He needed help. But he wouldn't let it go. Some deep-down instinct – must be his detective instinct – told him Ramon needed him.

If he had needed any more proof he had it now. She wouldn't let him in. Refused point-blank to let him see Ramon. He was sick, she said. Ha! As if he would believe that he was too sick to see him.

What more could he do? But he had to do something.

I was wasting time. I wanted to move on, felt an urgency to move on I couldn't explain. Time. It was all to do with time. Time running out. But even getting up to go to the toilet was an effort. As soon as I stood up my head reeled and I began to sway.

Bella came in at one point and offered to put a potty under the bed for me. That was the best cure for dizziness she could have come up with. No way.

'Sleep's the best thing, Ramon,' she said. 'You'll feel better tomorrow.'

But sleep wasn't helping me at all, because my sleep was full of dreams and they were all of the Dark Man coming to get me. Close, near. Where was he? And now,

81

he wasn't alone. There was someone else in the shadows, standing with the Dark Man; someone even scarier, and he was barring my way. And suddenly, there wasn't just one Dark Man; there was a thousand of them, a legion of them. And I was the only one who could stop them! I opened my eyes and there he was. The Dark Man.

He was in the room with me, standing in the shadows. I could see him. How did he get in here? *Nowhere to run now, Ram*, I thought, looking all around me for an escape. I leapt to my feet. He didn't move. He knew there was nowhere for me to go.

It was Mata to the rescue, for just at that moment she pawed at the door to get in and it swung open.

I didn't waste a second. I ran for the door, saw his hand reach out for me, but the door was between us now. I almost tripped on the stairs, tumbled and yelled. And he was there, gripping at my arm, turning me round. I began to fight him off; I wouldn't go down without a fight – he knew that.

'Get away from me!'

But he was stronger than I was. Much stronger. He was lifting me to my feet, carrying me. I struggled. I punched at him.

'No!'

'It's OK, Ramon, you're safe.'

I opened my eyes, out of my nightmare, and looked into blue eyes dotted with grey: the eyes of Catman. He smelt of grease and stale food, and his clothes clung to him with sweat. I thought he looked wonderful.

He wasn't the Dark Man. Yet I shot upright and looked all around, half thinking he would be there at the door – that they were all part of some conspiracy against me.

Catman followed my eyes. 'He's not here. You were dreaming. This Dark Man you're so afraid of isn't here.'

His voice was soft and reassuring. 'You need to get your memory back. There are people who know how to help you. Doctors. Psychiatrists.'

'No. I don't trust anyone. I just know I can't let him get me. I can't let Mr Death get me. I want to live, Catman.'

'Then I wish I could take your place. Mr Death can't come soon enough for me.'

His words stayed with me long after he had gone. *Death can't come soon enough for me.* They made me feel so sad. If only I knew what to say to Catman to help him.

18

What else could Ryan do? He had to help Ramon. He was genuinely worried about him, but he still hovered at his dad's study door, trying to decide whether he should knock or not.

Finally, it was his dad who hauled open the door and stood glaring down at him. 'Right! You've been hanging about there for long enough. What is wrong?'

So Ryan told him. The words mumbled and confused. 'I went to visit Ramon and she wouldn't let me in to see him, Dad.'

And he had an explanation for that. 'He's not well, like she told you. And I certainly don't want you catching whatever he's got. Fleas, probably.'

'But she let that tramp in. Catman. So he can't be that sick.'

'She's dotty, as you well know.'

And that was all Ryan needed his dad to say. 'But if she is so dotty, then maybe she doesn't realise what kind of man he really is – that he's a bad man. I just want to make sure Ramon's all right.'

84

Catman came back up to see me before he left that night. I felt better – weak, but the sweating was gone, the dreams and the hallucinations too. I was on the mend.

'I'll be on my way tomorrow,' he said.

I was beginning to think of when I could leave too, I told him.

'Well, make sure you get right away from this place. I don't want you going anywhere near Dobie's Doom. Will you promise me that?'

'Why should you care what I do? You're done with the human race, you said.'

His eyes crinkled into a smile. 'Maybe some of that optimism of yours is eating its way into my soul. But you're a good boy, and I don't want to see anything happen to you.'

'You've got a heart after all.' I smiled too.

He was having none of that. 'That's why I have to get away from you. You're a bad influence. I used to be like you, full of hope – and look where it got me. You're different though, special. I only wish you could hold on to that faith you have in people.'

I was chuffed with the compliment, but I didn't think I deserved it. 'What about Bella? She's a good sort, isn't she?'

He had to think about that. 'Even Bella's done things that don't bear thinking about,' he said.

'Bella?' I tried to imagine Bella doing anything like that. Couldn't. 'You sure you're not getting your Bellas mixed up.'

He tapped his nose. 'Bella has secrets. I know some of

them, but not everything. No one should know everything about a person. You've got to have some secrets.'

'I just wish I knew what mine were.'

'Why don't you just melt into the shadows, let this Dark Man know you're not a threat? Get on with your life?'

'I've got to stop something . . . Someone's relying on me. That's all I know. I can't let them down. And . . . I have to let my mum and dad know I'm still alive. They must think I'm dead already.' It seemed to me the only answer. 'That's why there's no one looking for me.' I was growing excited at the thought of it.

'You're a boy who won't let go of a mystery, eh?' He shook his head. 'Well, maybe at least I can solve one mystery for you. You really think you saw something in the valley?'

'I know I did. Strange lights, weird figures. Yeah, Catman – there's a mystery up there too.'

He smiled. 'How about I go up to this place – have a look around for you, see what I can see? I'll come back and tell you what I find. And if I find nothing, will you forget about it?'

'You'd do that for me?'

He only shrugged his big shoulders.

'You'll be careful, won't you?'

'Careful of what? Little green men?' He laughed.

'No,' I said. 'Something menacing up there. People disappearing. It's all connected, I'm sure of it. Please be careful.'

'Don't worry about me. I'm a big man.' He punched

his chest. 'I can take care of myself,' he said. 'I'll be sitting here eating one of Bella's breakfasts by the time you wake up in the morning – give you a full report. How about that?'

19

I was back in bed when I heard someone at the door. It was late.

Catman had gone; I wondered what he might find up there in the valley? Maybe nothing. At least I hoped so. Bella had been bustling about in the kitchen. I was feeling better – headache gone, and already making plans for moving on. My fever had gone too. I felt weak, but for the first time I was hungry – even for Bella's food.

I heard a man's voice and, for a second, I froze. Talking so much about the Dark Man, having him fill my nightmares for days and nights, I thought for a terrified moment that he had found me. He was here. He had tracked me to Bella's house. I would never get away from him.

I leapt up from the bed and listened at the door, my eyes darting about the room, looking for a quick exit. Then I heard Ryan's chirpy voice.

'Can I see him, then?'

He wasn't waiting for an answer. He was taking the stairs two at a time to get up to me. I opened the door to him.

His eyes went like moons with relief when he saw me.

'I thought they'd done something awful to you. I made my dad come and ask about you.' His glance shot downstairs.

I had to smile. 'You really are a detective, aren't you?'

'Told you. Nothing gets past me.' He closed the door. I could hear his dad apologising for his son rushing into the house without being invited. I could hear Bella's giggled reply. 'Boys will be boys.'

Was she fluttering her eyelashes again? Flirting with Ryan's dad? Wouldn't put it past her.

'I came earlier and she wouldn't let me in.'

'I know. She told me. I've been in bed all day.' I touched my brow. 'I had a fever. Feel better now.'

'Sure she didn't drug you?'

'I don't think she's the kind of person who goes about drugging people. My gran wouldn't do things like that.'

Ryan tried to backtrack. 'No, I didn't mean her . . . I meant that Catman. I've watched him. He's been here all day. I don't trust him.'

'Ryan, he couldn't have been nicer. Maybe you shouldn't judge people just by the way they look.'

His face flushed and I knew I had hurt his feelings. 'Me? I never judge people by the way they look. I don't trust him. Wouldn't care if he was dressed like a pop star! I don't judge your gran by the way she looks either. She looks like a daft old woman, and I don't think she is . . . I don't even think daft Lenny is as daft as he looks. That could all be an act. I've seen him sometimes, and he looks suspicious.'

And in that instant I remembered the dark look he had shot at Bella and I wondered too.

'I don't judge people by the way they look,' Ryan finished, his face grim.

And he was right. Maybe it was me who was judging people. Ryan saw the moment of doubt in my eyes. 'See, you think Catman might be up to something too!'

'No. He's just a vagabond.'

Ryan was having none of that. 'A vagabond! That's just a toff name for a tramp. A useless member of society. Don't you go be taken in by him. He's lulling you into a false sense of security. I read that in a book.'

His dad called up to him then. 'Ryan! Down here immediately.'

It was nice he came to check on me. I wanted him to know I appreciated it. 'Thanks, Ryan. I'm glad you came, but I'm fine. Honest.'

He looked around the room, almost as if he expected to spot some kind of bugging device – proof someone was listening into our conversation. 'If you need me, just come, won't you?'

Catman hauled his way up the hill, following the menacing path of Dobie's Doom. The waterfall was even more treacherous after so much rain. Still it poured down. He was soaked through and breathless. 'You're getting past it, old man,' he whispered to himself.

Why had he come here? Because of a promise to a boy he hardly knew? Catman wasn't usually one to keep promises. But there was something about that boy – his zest for life, when he could remember nothing of his past and all he knew was fear and uncertainty. Catman would check the place out, for the boy's sake – find nothing, of course, certainly not any little green men. He'd go back and tell him there was nothing here – an empty valley – and then he would move on. It was time for Catman to be off again. Too long in one place was bad for him.

And the boy would move on too. His memory would return. He would find the mother and father he longed for. Catman just didn't like the thought of the boy coming back here. To this place.

If he stopped once as he climbed to the brow of the hill, he stopped a dozen times – getting his breath, looking round, checking things out. Yet, what was he looking for? He couldn't say. But the boy thought there was something here, and he was sharp, that boy. He said he had seen something – strange figures, weird lights – and the boy wouldn't lie.

At last he reached the top of the hill. He looked down into the valley and saw only an expanse of grass and shrubs and trees merging into darkness. And the rain hammering down incessantly. Mist rising through the trees. Nothing out of place or strange. He moved down, looking all around him as he went, and then something did strike him as odd. There were no sounds. No sounds of the night, of birds or animals.

He turned quickly, sure for a moment there was something behind him. But there was nothing. Perhaps just some grass swishing in the wind and the rain.

He walked on. He wished there was a moon to shed some light, but it was dark now – clouds hanging so low they almost touched the trees. He wasn't afraid . . . but

91

he was apprehensive. It was as if someone was here, watching. He glanced round again. Even in the darkness there was nowhere for anyone to hide. He stood and made a circle, turning right round, letting his long coat billow about him. Nothing and no one. Yet, one step on, that same feeling. Something close behind him.

He spun round swiftly, sure this time he would catch whatever it was that was following him. But there was nothing. Nothing.

And then, coming from nowhere, rising into the night sky, a light. A ghostly green light. He blinked, wiped the rain from his eyes to see more clearly. He heard a sound at his back. He turned. And now there *was* something behind him. Close behind him. A face. But not a human face. Blank, no expression. Catman tried to take a step back. 'What the . . .'

20

THURSDAY

I woke early to the dullest, most miserable day you can imagine. The sky hung heavy and rain hammered against the window like spears. Yet, my heart felt good. I had figured something out. My mum and dad didn't know I was alive. I could almost picture them somewhere, grieving for me. I was going to beat the Dark Man, and then I was going to walk back into their lives. My prize for stopping whatever it was I was meant to stop. My happy ending.

I took a tentative step out of the bed and stood up. I waited for the room to sway around me, but it didn't. It was all the proof I needed. I was ready to move on.

Move on where? a voice inside me queried, and I didn't know the answer to that, as I didn't know the answer to so many things.

I tiptoed to the bathroom downstairs. No sign of Bella. Probably off on one of her mysterious trips on her bike. A shower, one of Bella's dubious breakfasts and, after I had spoken to Catman, I would go. Bella wouldn't stop me. She knew now I needed to move on. Had to keep one step ahead of the Dark Man.

Could I travel on with Catman? For a moment I imagined us together, living by our wits, going from place to place. Vagabonds together.

But the picture evaporated. Catman was a loner. He wouldn't want company. And I couldn't risk putting him in danger from the Dark Man.

No, I would go on alone.

Mata and Hari followed after me, winding themselves round my legs, looking for breakfast too. I wasn't going to get any peace till they were fed, so I searched in Bella's cupboards, found a tin of tuna and began looking for a can opener.

I opened one drawer after another, rummaging between bills and pens and cutlery, and dishtowels. No tin opener. Did this woman ever tidy her house? There was only one drawer left, the drawer in her computer desk. Stupid place to keep a can opener but then this was Bella. Who knew what she kept in those drawers?

I only hope it isn't her knickers, I was thinking as I pulled the drawer open . . . and stepped back.

I didn't find a can opener, but I did find something else.

A gun.

Bella had a gun in the drawer, hidden under a diary and a notebook and sheaves of paper. Bella had a gun. Daft old Bella had a gun. I stared at it for a long time. *Bella's done things that don't bear thinking about*, Catman had told me.

Who was Bella?

She definitely wasn't the daft old woman she seemed.

I heard the door open, and closed the drawer quickly, moved away from the desk. Bella came in the kitchen door, shaking herself like a wet dog. The cats saw her too and went bounding towards her, sure she would find them food quicker than I could.

'How are my honeys?' She patted the cats, then saw me standing there, fully dressed. 'How's my lovely Ramon?' she said as if I really was her beloved grandson. Was Ryan right? Was she really someone I should be afraid of? She came towards me and felt my brow. 'No temperature, and you look a lot better.'

'Feel better. I'm ready to move on,' I said, waiting for her to argue with that. But she didn't. She seemed distracted. 'As soon as I say goodbye to Catman, I'll be off, then.'

'Mmm, Catman,' she said. Then she hauled the curtain at the window across and peered outside. 'I'd have thought Catman would be back by now . . . especially on a morning like this.'

Ryan was going to be bold today. He was going to pop in and see Ramon before he went to school. He pushed open the creaky old gate leading to the alien queen's front door and walked up the path.

He had a good excuse. He wanted to check how Ramon was feeling this morning.

To his surprise, it was Ramon himself who came to the front door.

'Hi,' Ryan said. 'You look worse than you did last night.'

95

Ramon's smile was weak. But Ryan thought he looked thinner, paler. 'Thanks for that,' he said. He glanced back into the house, as if he was afraid. Something was bothering him. What was he hiding? Ryan was sure something was going on. Every detective instinct he had told him that.

'Something's wrong, isn't it?' he whispered. He knew it had to be to do with the old woman. 'I wish you would tell me.'

'Why should something be wrong?' Ramon asked, but it was almost as if he was asking himself that question.

'I'm a detective – I know these things.'

Ramon smiled, though Ryan couldn't see that he'd said anything funny.

'I'll probably be going home later, Ryan. I might not see you again.'

Ryan didn't like the sound of that at all. Ramon goes. He can't get in touch with him. Another person disappearing. How would he know if he had gone home or become another victim?

'Couldn't you wait till lunchtime? I could come home then, have my lunch with you.'

'Depends,' Ramon said.

'Depends on what?' Ryan asked.

'I'm waiting for Catman. He said he'd come back and he hasn't.'

Ryan wanted to say that was daft. Catman wouldn't come back, he hoped. But Ramon seemed to like him, so instead he changed the subject.

'How can I reach you? I'd like to keep in touch.' This

was his way of finding out if Ramon really had gone home.

It seemed to him that Ramon had to think about that. 'Maybe I will wait till you come home for lunch. I'm going to wait for Catman anyway.'

21

Catman woke in the dark – pitch-black, blacker than night. His head ached. He tried to sit up but he was held down, chained down like an animal. Where was he? He moved back and hit a cold steel wall. It was freezing here. But where was here? He waited for his eyes to become accustomed to the dark. And finally he was sure he could make out a vague shape close by. Alive, moving.

'Who's there?' he called. 'Who is that?'

The dark shape moved closer. It was that face again, that same blank face.

The voice when it came sounded unreal, high-pitched, inhuman. 'My name is the Reaper.'

I wanted to ask her where she had got the gun. Why did she need a gun? But all I did was watch her. Bella fumbled about the kitchen, searching for tea bags – found some in what looked like a toilet-roll holder.

'That's a nosy boy, that Ryan,' she muttered.

'You know, he's not such a bad detective,' I told her. 'He thinks people are going missing too. And he suspects I'm not your grandson. Maybe you two should get together, solve the mystery,' I said.

'That would just be perfect. Me and Ryan Gallacher. Miss Marple and Sherlock Holmes, I don't think.'

I was going to ask her who this Miss Marple was – one of her old friends maybe – but Bella had a question of her own. 'Where are you moving on to?'

I didn't answer for a moment. I watched her as she lifted the kettle from the hob and began filling her cat-shaped teapot.

She answered the question herself. 'Away from this Dark Man.' She seemed preoccupied and kept glancing out of the window. She was looking for Catman too.

'It's still early,' I pointed out. Though it was bothering me that he wasn't here yet.

'Half the day's gone for Catman. Up with the larks, he is.' She checked her wrist as if she wore a watch there. 'He's late.'

Maybe he's moved on too, I wondered.

But he had promised me he would come back, tell me what he had found up there in the valley. Give me a full report, he had said. And though I hardly knew him, I was sure he would have kept his word about that.

He had obviously promised Bella too. 'He said he'd be here for breakfast. He wouldn't leave without saying goodbye to me.'

I wondered then if Catman was another of her fantasy romances. But still, it bothered both of us. Where was Catman?

He still hadn't come by lunchtime. 'Another one missing,' Bella said finally. 'I warned him. I tried to warn him.'

'You don't know he's missing,' I said.

'That's what the police will say if I tell them. I'm a silly old woman and he's a vagabond. Comes and goes when he pleases.'

She didn't believe that. By now, neither did I.

'I'm going to go out for a while,' she said. 'See if anyone has seen him. You wait here till I come back. Can't worry about two of you, can I?'

I watched her cycle off down the street, the silly old woman back again. She was genuinely worried about Catman. So was I now. Why hadn't he come back? And the thought came to me: maybe he couldn't.

22

Ryan was out the school gates and hurrying towards Bella's while the school bell was still ringing. He had assured his teacher that he was allowed to go home for lunch today, as his mother would be home. If his dad found out he was telling lies to a teacher he would go spare.

But he would never find out. Ryan would hurry to Bella's and then race back to school. He had to see Ramon, make sure he was all right.

He went round to the side door; it was lying half open. She never seemed to lock her door. He knocked once, but there was no response, so he stepped into the kitchen. Crammed on every available surface there was junk, open jam jars, dishes and bags of potatoes. He thought of his own neat, tidy, clean house. He would hate to live like this. He moved through the kitchen and into the living room. Just as untidy. Magazines and books piled high on every chair. Discarded clothes, dirty cups and saucers, framed photographs, boxes of junk.

Framed photographs? Photographs always tell a story, he had read once. Ryan lifted one of them. It was Bella all right – young, her eyes bright. She was wearing a

101

uniform. Probably a traffic warden, Ryan thought. There was another photograph beside it. Bella again, this time an older Bella, and it looked as if she was getting some kind of medal. Her retirement most likely. He looked at all the other photographs in the room. Not one of Ramon. Now, that was suspicious. Not one photograph of her beloved grandson? Ryan thought of his own house. His photograph was everywhere: on the walls, in the hall, on top of the mantelpiece. It was embarrassing at times. But Bella didn't have a single one of Ramon.

He was still studying one of the photographs when he heard a sound behind him. He jumped round.

'Every heard of knocking?' It was Ramon.

'I did. No one answered.'

Ramon shrugged. 'I was in the loo.'

Ryan put the photo down, said the thing he was thinking. 'Your gran doesn't have one photo of you. How come?'

Ram lifted the photographs too, looked at them, one by one. He seemed to be studying them. Ryan was sure he was taking time to think up an answer. 'I hate getting my photo taken,' he said finally. Didn't seem like any kind of answer to Ryan.

'Why didn't you shout for me?' Ramon asked.

'I was detecting,' Ryan answered, and that made Ramon smile.

'Well, I just might have a mystery for you,' he said.

'A mystery? Wow! What is it?'

'I think Catman really has disappeared.'

Ryan threw himself on the settee. A pile of magazines

slid to the floor. 'Is that it?'

'Don't sound so disappointed. He went off last night, up to the valley. Said he'd be here first thing this morning . . . and he hasn't come.'

'He's a tramp. He's moved on,' Ryan said.

'Maybe he's one of your missing persons. Isn't that what everyone says about the people who've disappeared – that there's a logical reason for them going off? But just maybe something's happened to him.'

'Who cares about Catman, though?'

Ramon looked puzzled by that. Ryan tried to explain. 'He's only an old tramp. No good to anybody. He eats rats. He's dirty.'

'But even if all of those things were true, Ryan, wouldn't you still want to help him? He's a human being.'

'Questionable,' Ryan said.

'If you're really going to be a detective, you're going to have to help all kinds of people.'

Ryan thought about that. Of course he wanted to be a detective, to bring justice to the world. But he still thought he didn't want to help lowlifes like Catman. He could tell Ramon was puzzled. Or was that disappointment in his face?

'I came home from school to make sure you were OK,' he said. He wanted Ramon to see that he was one of the good guys. That he could depend on him. Ramon smiled.

'Thanks, but I'm fine.'

'Are you really going home?'

He seemed to think about that. 'I have to,' he said.

'But first I want to find out what happened to Catman.'

'But why?' Ryan asked.

'He went to the valley for me.' Ramon told him. 'That first night I saw something strange there.'

Ryan's heart leapt. 'You too? I knew it!'

'I don't know what it was – lights and some weird figures.'

Ryan slapped his head dramatically. 'Oh wow! You saw aliens. You must have. I knew they were out there. I've seen the lights too, Ramon, but nobody ever believes me.'

'Catman went to take a look. I think he was worried I might go back. He said he'd check it out for me and come back and set my mind at rest that there was nothing suspicious up there. But he hasn't come back.'

Ryan shrugged. 'That's just Catman, though. You can't trust him.'

'But I think I could, Ryan.'

He really believed that. Ryan could see that in Ramon's face, hear it in his voice.

He really trusted Catman.

Ramon turned his eyes to the window, as if he could see beyond the rain and the hills and the trees. As if he could see that valley. 'What is going on there?'

I watched Ryan hurry back to school. I had thought of asking him to go with me, just up to the valley, just to have a look. But his attitude to Catman bothered me. I supposed it was understandable. Weird guy comes and goes, legends start emerging about him. Catman was like the bogeyman. Ryan had probably been warned to stay well clear. But Catman wasn't just some old tramp. I knew that. He was something more, and I was sure he wouldn't just leave without coming back and telling me what he had found.

Like Bella, I had a gut feeling that something was wrong. Bella was looking for him in the town. But I was going to go looking for him over there in the valley. I was going back.

23

Catman was alone now. Not tied down any more. He had been drugged. It was wearing off, but he still had that thick, dry taste in his mouth and the heaviness in his head. He got to his feet unsteadily. Where was he? He began to feel his way along the walls – hard, metal walls. He couldn't even find a door. He called out, 'Is anyone there?' But there was no answer from the darkness. He had expected none. Finally, he sank back on to the camp bed.

A horrifying thought came to him. Maybe he was dead. Maybe this was hell. A pitch-black room with no exit.

That strange shadowy figure had called himself the Reaper. Wasn't that another name for Death?

Well, then, he'd finally got what he'd been longing for, hadn't he? Death.

He lay down on the bed, stared into the darkness. And Catman was afraid.

Bella was worried as she hurried back to her cottage. No one had seen Catman since yesterday. He had left her house and . . . *whoof* . . . he had disappeared into thin air. Just like the others. Of course, no one but her was worried about him.

It was exactly what she had feared, that if he came back to this town, he would be the next.

'Ramon!' She called his name as she opened the door, but there was a deathly silence in the house. Mata and Hari looked up at her lazily, but she knew right away the boy had gone.

She'd bet money he'd gone back up into the valley, and it was dangerous there. Why did he have to be such a hero?

If neither of them came back how could she make anyone listen to her? A tramp and a runaway boy? She would wait anyway. Wait until dark. But if he wasn't back, then she was going to use her last resort – again. She was going to call the only people left who could help her.

But this time she would make someone listen.

I trudged towards the valley. It was a miserable day. The rain came down as if someone had emptied a giant bucket of water over the earth. I headed for the only landmark I could find. Dobie's Doom. Heard it before I found it.

The water surged even more violently now as it gushed down into that dark tunnel. I stayed well back from the edge and kept climbing.

I stopped for a moment and stood under some trees as I surveyed the valley below. Bushes dripped with rain. Had he come here? And how would I know?

The ground was sodden and my feet squelched every time I took a step. There was nothing here, but I wouldn't give up. Catman had said he was coming here, and now he was gone. He had promised me he would come back, and he hadn't. I was sure he would have if it had been possible.

Something, or someone, had stopped him. I wasn't leaving here till I found some clue about what had happened to him.

It was growing dark already, even in the early afternoon – a grey day turning to black. The heavy clouds hung low, iron-grey in the sky. Soon it would be dusk and I wouldn't be able to see anything. I stood and looked all around me. There was nowhere here anyone could hide. Not for long. Bushes, boulders, grass, that was all. And if Catman had come here . . . why hadn't he come back?

Common sense told me I should leave. Everyone was right. Ryan was right. Catman was a vagabond. He had simply moved on.

Who thought otherwise? Only the dottiest person in town, Bella Bartell . . . and me.

Then, as I stood scanning the landscape, it occurred to me: something was different. But I couldn't figure out what.

Wait a minute . . . I shook the rain from my eyes and blinked. I was seeing things. Because the grass was moving, the bush was rising. It was the wind, I told myself. Had to be the wind. Or maybe my dizziness back again, suddenly coming over me like a wave. But my head was clear. I had no fever. I began to step forward slowly.

The ground had gone. I was staring into a black hole.

24

Ryan made a detour round the edge of the town. He wanted to see if Ramon was still there. He could see Bella in her kitchen. She seemed to be talking to someone, but there was no one there that he could see. *Daft as a brush*, he thought. It took all his courage – and, after all, a detective has to have courage – to knock at the door of her house. He took a step back, just in case she reached out a long, sharp-nailed hand and dragged him inside.

Instead, the door opened with a creak, and Bella Bartell peeked out.

'Yes, what do you want?' she asked.

Ryan coughed and tried to sound bold. 'Is Ramon still here?'

She didn't answer at once – as if she didn't know. Now that was suspicious, he thought. That would go down in his notebook. She rattled her teeth disgustingly. 'No, he went home this morning.'

A lie. She was telling him a lie. Ramon had been there at lunchtime. He hoped she couldn't read his mind, which was racing. Something was very wrong here.

'Is he feeling better, then?'

She smiled at him. 'Nice of you to ask. He's OK. I wouldn't have let him go home otherwise.' She began to close the door on him.

'Can I keep in touch? Has he got an email address?'

That took her by surprise. 'An email address? No.'

'Can I phone him?'

She surely couldn't say he didn't have a phone.

'I can never remember his number,' she said.

'If you give me his address I'll write to him.' She wouldn't dare say she didn't have her own grandson's address.

'I'll look it out for you,' she said.

Ryan didn't move.

'Not right now. I'm busy.'

She closed the door. Ryan stood staring at the wood for a moment. Ramon was gone. But his grandmother was acting as if she didn't know anything about where he was. Or perhaps didn't want to tell.

People in this town go missing, Ryan was thinking. Maybe now Ramon was missing. Ramon had told him Catman was missing too. But maybe – his mind shook with this horrible thought – maybe Catman had taken him.

Ramon might have trusted Catman, but Ryan certainly didn't.

He had to do something about this . . . But what?

I looked all around the valley. There was nothing to see. The mist rose from the ground, merged with the low clouds, draped itself around the trees. But there was no sign of anything human . . . or even not so human. Then I stared again down into the blackness below. The hole had been covered by a hatch. I didn't see it immediately as it was camouflaged by bushes, and when it rose, the bushes rose with it. Anyone watching it rise could easily mistake it for the wind. It must have opened only a second ago. I had walked this way, walked right past it and had seen no sign of it. I knelt down, felt the soft ground all around the hole. Now I could see there were metal steps leading down. The rungs seemed to disappear into the blackness below. Did I dare go down?

My common sense told me it was a trap. Someone had opened the hatch. Someone must have known I was there. Yet I couldn't stop myself from taking that first step. I would just have a quick look, see where those steps led. I took another step, then one more, reluctant to leave even the dimming light from the sky.

'Is anybody there?' My voice echoed eerily into the dark. This was madness. No one knew where I was. What if I were to be trapped down there? I'd be lost for ever in the dark. I had a sudden picture of myself dangling in eternal space. I felt the sweat begin to drip down my back.

What should I do? The sensible thing would be to go back to Bella, tell her about my discovery . . . let her inform the police; let them investigate what was down there. For once, I decided, I would do the sensible thing.

I had been a fool even taking those first few steps.

I felt better when I'd made that decision. I began to pull myself back up . . . and an arc of darkness cut across the grey sky. The hatch was closing.

I've never moved so fast, almost slipping on the steps, racing to reach the sky, to slide through, back into the open air.

I could make it, I knew I could. My foot slipped, my hand slipped, but I reached the top.

A second too late. The sky disappeared.

25

Bella waited till the boy, Ryan, had gone, though it had taken him an age to leave, kicking stones all down the path, dragging his rucksack. He had known something was wrong, the little detective. He hadn't believed her, but he didn't know what to do about it.

Neither did she.

The boy was not her grandson, so how could she go to the police to say he was missing after she had pretended that he was? Too many questions. She'd be in real trouble then. A runaway boy, they would say, who had simply run off again.

And Catman, the same story. An itinerant, a vagabond, who never stayed long anywhere.

And the police were sick of hearing her wild stories. They never took her seriously.

But there were other people she could call. There was a time when they had listened to her. She would make them listen again.

Outside, darkness had fallen. She had waited long enough. She was reluctant to make this call, but now she had no other choice.

Bella began to dial.

I was dizzy with fear. I was in total blackness. I pounded on the roof of the hatch and it rang metallically. I yelled. I shouted. But I hadn't the strength to push it up. Someone had closed it on me deliberately. Someone wanted me trapped down here.

Where was here?

I hung in mid-air, imagination bringing strange things up from the darkness below. Wet, black tentacles reaching out for my legs, winding their way towards me, so real I tucked my legs up on the next rung.

I shouted again. 'Help!' But my voice was a whimper.

I wrapped my arms around the metal rung of the ladder and tried to think.

OK, I had got myself into this situation. Now how was I going to get myself out of it?

I tried to think logically, to put the thought of the darkness and what could be hiding within it to the very back of my mind.

I couldn't go up. I couldn't stay here for ever. *No choice, Ram*, I told myself. *You have to go down*.

This was no ordinary hole. It had been manufactured: a metal lid, a metal ladder leading down. Man-made. At least, I hoped it was man-made. Anything not of this world I couldn't cope with. The steps had to lead somewhere.

I went down.

It seemed I went down for ever. I tried to count the rungs, lost count after twenty. Down and down. My legs ached and so did my arms, I held on so tightly to the rungs as I descended.

There was no sound here. Underground. Nothing.

The black water at the bottom took me by surprise. I almost fell into it. The steps sunk beneath it. But I could make out solid ground nearby. I leapt towards it. The soles of my feet stung with the force of my landing, and I stood for a moment, getting my breath back, listening for any other sound. Nothing.

Now I was here, what would I do?

Try to find a way out, you idiot!

But which way?

My eyes had grown accustomed to the dark. I could make out just how big this chamber was: black as death, but with long corridors stretching out like claws. One in front of me, one to the left and one to the right. What was this place?

And how was I going to get out of this one?

How long would he be here? For eternity? That would indeed be hell. Catman would never see the sun again, or the moon. His family would never find out what had happened to him.

Would they care?

He remembered his father. That bitter, angry man, alienating Catman and his sisters. He had watched him treat his family like dirt, treat his employees even worse, ruin people's lives all for the sake of money, and he had grown to hate his father. He didn't want to live like him; wanted nothing of his. Because of his father, his sister had cut short her own life, and that had been the end for

Catman. In spite of his other sisters' pleas, he had gone; wanted nothing to do with his family, or life. And since then, he hadn't seen anything to make him change his mind about that.

Men greedy for money.

Wars, conspiracies, genocide. The world falling apart.

And then he had met the boy.

The boy who believed there was so much good in the world. The boy with no memory but a faith in human beings, and so desperate to find a family.

Catman had promised to come back. He hoped the boy wouldn't think he had broken that promise.

26

The Reaper had the boy trapped. It had been so easy. The boy was curious, and everyone knew that curiosity killed the cat. Well, it hadn't killed him – yet. The Reaper watched him closely – the darkness was no problem. The Reaper belonged in the dark. The boy hesitated, didn't know which way to go. Whichever way, he was trapped. He was in the Reaper's power now. The boy circled round, almost as if he could hear the Reaper's breath behind him. There was fear in his movements – fear of the dark, fear of the unknown. But then the boy stood straight: a decision had been made. He moved on.

The Reaper waited only a moment, then softly – he was so used to not making a sound – he followed after him.

Ryan didn't go home. He left Bella's and, without thinking, headed out of the town using the shortcut across the fields that led to the valley. He had seen the lights here: strange, green lights. No one ever believed him. But Ramon had seen them too, and more. Strange figures, alien figures. Catman, he said, had come up here

. . . and hadn't come back.

The rain was like needles against his face and he pulled the hood of his jacket tighter under his chin. His mother would be home soon, wondering where he was. He was always supposed to come straight home after school. But Ryan felt sure Ramon was in trouble. He had been worried about Catman. Maybe he had gone back to the valley to find him.

He was panting by the time he reached the crest of the hill. Usually Ryan loved days like this. Gloomy, dark days, full of mist and rain. He walked on. His eyes scanned the ground for clues – some sign that Ramon had been here.

It was a waste of time! The rain would have washed everything away.

Then, just as he was about to turn to go home, he saw the footprints. Same size as his. A boy's footprints, embedded into the soft earth.

Going nowhere.

Now, this was strange. The footsteps were there – he could still see traces of them, as if the owner, like him, had been searching around this place – and then, suddenly, they were gone, as if . . . He looked up. Ryan's eyes scanned the heavy skies.

As if he had been lifted up.

Abducted.

Aliens. It was surely the only possible explanation.

He stepped back.

Well, they weren't going to get him too. He began to run, hardly daring to look behind him. He had never run so fast. All the time he was thinking about the people going missing. Catman going missing. And now Ramon. All linked with this valley. He had found the clue.

They had all been taken up by aliens. That was the only answer.

But who should he tell? Who would believe him?

I stepped gingerly further into the tunnel. My foot hit against something hard. I bent down and my fingers closed on some kind of metal bar. I lifted it. It could come in handy as a weapon if I needed one. There had to be another way out of here, surely – I had to hold on to that thought. The tunnels went off in different directions. I didn't know which one to follow.

Was this place man-made?

Or . . . ? I couldn't stop thinking of the stories of alien spacecraft, the sightings, this area being the UFO capital of the country. I remembered the weird figures I had seen.

Up there in the open air, on planet earth, all that had seemed stupid, unbelievable. But now, down here, I didn't know what to think.

I swivelled round again. Was someone there, hiding in the darkness? I'd had a feeling since I came down here that I was not alone.

'Is there anybody there?' My voice didn't come out as strong as I wanted it to. A tinny shadow of a voice. It sounded as scared as I felt.

There was no answer. Had I expected there to be?

But just as I turned to move on, I heard it behind me. It sounded like a laugh – a tremor of laughter that slithered towards me like a snake. I could almost feel it coming closer.

Someone was there, or something. And it was laughing at me.

I didn't wait to find out what it was. I began to run.

27

Ryan found himself back outside Bella Bartell's house. It seemed his feet had automatically taken him there. Did that mean he should tell her what he was thinking?

Or was he only here because he thought she was the one person daft enough to believe him?

He stood at her gate. The rain was still pouring down, running down his face, dripping from his nose. He was wet through. He stood watching her front door, half hoping she might suddenly fling it open and confront him. And what would he say then? 'Your grandson's been taken by aliens'?

He finally pushed open the gate, walked warily up the path. Then he stood at the front door, trying to pluck up the courage to knock.

He couldn't bring himself to do it. It was as if his arm was paralysed, refused to do his bidding. He'd go round the side, he decided. Give himself some more time to think what he would say to Bella. It was misty dark outside as Ryan passed her living-room window. Lights were just beginning to come on in the town. But Bella's house was in darkness. Almost in darkness.

It was the green light that made him stop.

He hid at the side of the window and dared a glance inside. There she was, Bella Bartell. She didn't even see him. She was too intent on what she was doing to notice him. And suddenly, she didn't look dotty any more. She was concentrating on the screen of her computer. (Bella Bartell had a computer . . . and knew how to work it?!) Her fingers were flying over the keys, her eyes never moving from the screen. The green light gave her face an eerie glow.

That was the thing that decided Ryan. This wasn't the same daft old Bella that everyone knew. This was someone different – almost as if she had been taken over by another personality . . . He'd seen that in a film once. Dr Jekyll and Mr Hyde.

Taken over. The words repeated themselves in his head.

She had come here from nowhere. No one knew who she was. Perhaps she had been brought here. He had always suspected that was the case. But perhaps she hadn't always been an alien. Perhaps in one of her lone visits to the valley, she had been taken over. She had come back a different person.

Ryan swivelled round, sure he heard a sound behind him. Sure for a moment he might see Ramon standing behind him, and he would be different too.

There was no way he could confide in Bella. He'd have to think of something else. Bella Bartell was just too weird.

I was underground in the dark, running, and it occurred

to me that there was no life down here at all. No spiders, no scurrying rats. No sound. It was as if this place had been sealed tight – or was there something else down here preventing any form of life? I stopped for breath. Listened. Heard nothing.

Did anyone know this place existed – hidden deep in the earth, tunnels and chambers and sealed rooms? What was this place?

An underground bunker.

The words came to me easily. This was an underground bunker.

People had been disappearing. What better place to hide them than down here? But why?

I thought of Catman, somewhere in these dark tunnels.

Wondered if I dared to call for him.

Or was I just being stupid? There was a logical explanation for all the disappearances: a girl had run off with a boyfriend, a man with another man's wife, Catman had simply gone off as he always did . . .

What was I doing here?

I moved on, treading carefully. I had turned at least two corners as I ran. I prayed I would be able to find my way back, wouldn't be lost in the darkness for ever.

I had to get out. Even if there was something here, how could I ever find it without a light? If I came down again, I would bring a torch . . .

If I came down again! As if! Nothing would bring me into this black hellhole again. Once I found a way out I was never coming back. If something, someone, was down here . . . I would let other people discover them.

The boy was moving past the door. If he had known it was a door, tried to open it – well, what delights were behind that door! Home of the Guardians.

He was looking for a way out and there was only one. Maybe one other, but that way would lead to almost certain death.

That might be fun too, the Reaper decided.

There was water now, getting deeper with every step I took. I wouldn't be able to go much further. I would have to go back. Could I find my way out? I turned, began walking back along the corridor, feeling my way along the walls, afraid of what my hand might touch. Something oozing through the walls, reaching out to me. Just my imagination, I told myself.

If there were people down here, how would I know? My voice only echoed through the tunnels and came back to me, bouncing off the metal doors and walls.

Metal. An idea came to me. Metal against metal. Surely that sound would reverberate through all these tunnels. No matter where he might be, if Catman was here, he would surely hear it. I lifted the metal bar in my hand and hit it against the wall as hard as I could, listened for a moment, then hit it again. There was nothing. No answer. I waited. All was silence. This was stupid. But I would try it again, one more time.

28

'What on earth are you doing with my kitchen foil, Ryan?' His mother came into his room, taking him completely by surprise. He hadn't thought she'd be back from work so soon.

'I'm making . . .' he hesitated. How could he tell her he was making foil caps to prevent them being abducted by aliens? Three of them. One for him, one for his dad and one for his mum. He had seen a film where the foil acted as protection against alien mind control.

'It's a school project, Mum,' he said. 'Do you mind?'

'Of course not,' she said. She was understanding, his mum, Ryan thought, and he was tempted to confide in her there and then. *Ramon has been abducted. I found his footprints and then . . . they were gone.* She would inform the proper authorities – they would be able to do something, surely?

She came across and peered at his handiwork. 'Looks like a spaceship. It's not one of those stupid alien projects again, is it?'

She didn't wait for an answer. She was more amused than annoyed. 'Dinner will be ready soon,' she said. Then she was gone, and the moment passed. He crumpled the foil in his hand. Stupid idea! Of course he couldn't confide in his mum, or his dad. Definitely not his dad. They thought it was all rubbish. They would never believe him.

The aliens were here and they had his friend.

He would have to find someone else to help him.

Catman leapt to his feet. The sound echoed outside, seemed to scream towards him. He ran to the wall. Listened. The sound suddenly reverberated against his ear. Someone was out there. Someone had come to help.

He had a sudden picture of the boy. Why? Couldn't possibly be him. The police, the army, maybe – but not the boy. Yet the image wouldn't go away: the boy, alone, come to his aid.

The sound came again. Help was out there, waiting. But he needed an answer. Catman felt around and his hand found the tin bucket, lying somewhere in a corner. He gripped it, lifted it and crashed it against the wall. Not once, not twice, but over and over. The boy had to hear him. He had to be out there. Stay. Help.

He was breathless when he stopped. He leant against the wall, sweat pouring from him, and he waited.

He was here! I almost yelled with delight when I heard the sound. At first I'd thought it was an echo, but this was no echo. This was a desperate cry for freedom. Where was he? Somewhere behind those steel walls. I followed the sound, wanted to find the corridor it was

127

coming from. Catman was inside one of those sealed chambers. Trapped.

And then, his clanging was joined by another . . . and then another, till the tunnels rang with the wild sound of it. And I knew in that second they were all here – all trapped here somewhere. I wanted to help them. I had to help them, but how?

Catman heard it too, an answering call, and then another. He wasn't alone. They were all here – all the missing people – in cells just like this, trapped inside steel. He began to ram the bucket even harder against the wall till he could feel it begin to crumple with the force of it. His heart was almost bursting, for he suddenly realised, with a joy he couldn't control, that he wasn't in hell.

He wasn't dead.

He was alive.

29

Ryan walked into the local police station. He had come on his bike, sneaking out of the house after dinner while his dad was in his study and his mum was on the phone. It had taken him a long time to pluck up the courage to walk inside. He had spent ages going through all the options he had.

Tell Bella? No way. He had always suspected there was something fishy about her. Now he was sure the truth was that she had been abducted by aliens herself and was no longer the real Bella Bartell, but some kind of alien replacement.

Not his mum, she would only laugh.

And definitely not his dad. His dad was so preoccupied at the moment, always in his study working. Ryan had tried to talk to him after dinner, had almost blurted out what he wanted to say, but it wouldn't come. He could see his dad's mind was somewhere else. There was a big promotion coming at work – Ryan had heard his mum and dad talking about it. It would mean big changes, and his dad had to be 'up to the job', he kept saying. Ryan knew how much the job meant to him, and as he watched his dad walking back into his study and closing the door, he realised he would be better leaving this in the hands of the professionals. People who were used to dealing with this kind of thing. He would make them believe him.

So here he was at the police station.

He stepped inside through the automatic doors. The posters on the walls were all warning the public to be aware of crime.

DO NOT LEAVE ITEMS UNATTENDED OR THEY COULD BE CONFISCATED AND DESTROYED.

Ryan thought about his bike lying at the bottom of the stairs outside. He hoped they wouldn't think it was some kind of unexploded bomb.

'Yes, young man?' The policeman, appearing from some kind of office behind the desk, made Ryan jump. He took a step forward.

'I'd like to report a missing person.'

The policeman, younger than Ryan had expected, leant over the desk. 'Who?'

'His name's Ramon . . . I think it might be Ramon Bartell. He's Bella Bartell's grandson.'

At the mention of Bella Bartell's name the policeman blew out his cheeks.

'She says he's gone home.' Ryan kept talking. 'But he hasn't.' Now was the big moment. Ryan took a deep breath. 'But I know where he is.'

'Well, if you know where he is, he's not missing, is he?'

He kind of smiled at that, as if he expected Ryan to see the joke.

'This isn't funny,' Ryan said. 'He's been abducted by aliens.'

The policeman let out a moan and rolled his eyes. 'Not another one,' he said. 'I've already had someone in here saying a flying saucer's just landed on his front lawn.' He looked at the calendar. 'Is it April the first yet?'

Ryan knew he was making it up. He gripped the counter with both hands. 'I was up there in the valley. I followed his footprints . . . and then they suddenly just disappeared. As if he'd been . . .'

Ryan didn't say anything else. He looked up. The policeman looked up too. Then he looked back at Ryan. Now he wasn't smiling.

'And where did you say this was?'

'The valley, up near Dobie's Doom. I could show you the exact spot. Something's happened up there. Please. Please, say you'll investigate.'

The policeman still looked at him. 'And what's your name and address?'

Ryan was reluctant to give it, but he had no choice.

'You wait here, young man. We'll get it all sorted.'

'Will you? You promise?' Ryan asked.

'You see if we don't,' the policeman said.

Ryan took a seat against the wall. He felt better now. He had told the police and they would do something about it. Ramon would be found. Safe and well.

The Reaper was not pleased. He listened to the cacophony of sound in growing anger. They had never known anyone else was here – each of them in their own separate little soundproof container. Until that boy came.

131

He had thought about keeping the boy. He would have been a useful subject. Now, perhaps it was better if he found out exactly what was down here. Perhaps it was time to unleash his own final solution.

I began to hurry towards the corridor where all the sounds were coming from. They were all here. All the missing people. I couldn't think how or why. Didn't matter; they were here and I could help them.

But there seemed to be no doors and there was no light. It was as if they were all locked inside the walls. I needed help.

Then I heard it: another ominous noise along the dark corridor. I couldn't make out a thing, but something was up there in the dark. Something swishing rhythmically towards me out of the blackness, heading my way.

Ever had that feeling of terror when you can't see what's coming but you know it might be your worst nightmare?

30

Ten minutes later, Ryan's dad walked into the police station. Ryan jumped to his feet. His dad's face was like thunder, as if a dark cloud had settled on his features. 'Oh, Ryan! What do you think you're playing at?'

The policeman came round the desk. He was smiling. 'Thought we'd better let you know, Mr Gallacher.'

'Aliens again!' his dad said.

His mum hurried in behind him. She held out one of the foil caps. 'So that's why you were making these?' She sounded even more annoyed than his dad.

Ryan was mortified. He looked at the policeman. 'I thought you'd help. You're supposed to help.'

'They did,' his dad said. 'They phoned me. Now come on.'

'Boys will be boys,' the young policeman said. That almost made Ryan laugh, seeing as he was hardly more than a boy himself. 'Especially in this crazy town.'

His dad manhandled him out of the police station. Ryan tried to pull away from him but his grip was tight.

'You embarrassed me, Dad.'

'I embarrassed you?' His dad let out a long sigh. 'I have to come to the police station to get you because

you've been saying someone's been abducted by aliens –
and you think I'm the one who's embarrassed you!'

'We're not the kind of family who gets involved with
the police,' his mum said. She pushed his bike angrily
into the back of the car.

'Especially now. You know I have a big promotion
coming up,' his dad said.

Was that all they cared about?

'Ramon's disappeared,' Ryan muttered.

'He's gone home,' his dad told him.

Ryan sat silently in the back of the car as they drove
home. Why didn't they understand?

His dad pulled into their drive. He hadn't said a word
all the way. 'Tomorrow I'll go to Bella Bartell's and ask
about her grandson. How about that?'

Ryan wanted to tell him that would be no help at all.
She was one of them now. But if they didn't believe him
when he said Ramon had been abducted, then they
wouldn't believe him about anything else. 'OK,' he said.

His mum patted his shoulder, her anger gone. 'And
from now on, if you need help, please ask us, not the
police.'

His dad repeated that solemnly. 'No. Not the police,
Ryan.'

'Who's there?' I shouted it.

The swish-swish – that sound – didn't miss a beat.

I began to run, down the corridor towards the hatch.
Something wicked this way comes . . . Had I heard that
phrase before, or had I just made it up? But something

134

wicked was definitely coming my way.

And still it came closer.

I was back at the metal steps leading up to the ground! I leapt towards the bottom rung and climbed. I banged on the hatch like a madman, pushed with all my strength, my eyes darting below me. That sound was getting closer and closer. I called out – shouted until my throat ached; battered against the hatch till my arms were exhausted.

It was no use. I could never get that hatch open. I hated the dark. Hated not being able to see what was following me. I could still hear the clanging through the tunnels, but never as loud as that unearthly sound somewhere below.

I had to get away. I'd find help. Send someone back. But I had to get away from that sound.

I looked down into the black water below me. Could that lead to the outside? No. I didn't dare try that way.

I recognised the rising feeling of utter terror. Had felt it before.

I began pushing frantically at the hatch again. It was useless. I yelled even louder for help, but there was no one who could help me down here.

And still it came closer.

What was making that sound? Anything human? Why couldn't I see?

Where could I go?

The black water beckoned me. Where did it lead? Anywhere? Well, I wasn't staying put and waiting for whatever was heading for me to get me.

I took a deep breath, and dived.

31

The Reaper slammed down the gate in front of the Guardians. They were too precious to lose in the dark water. Couldn't risk losing them.

Who was this boy? He had been a challenge. But he had taken the only other way out. He had jumped into the black water. He didn't know where that black water would take him, drag him. But the Reaper knew.

And it was certain death.

If only he could capture it on film.

No more sounds. Catman stopped banging. Listened. They had all stopped, waiting. But there were no more sounds.

Had he been caught? Was he safe?

The boy. The image of him wouldn't leave his mind. The boy would be back.

He imagined them all in their cells, just like his, hope draining from them, thinking they had been abandoned. They needed to hold on to hope. The hope that they would be rescued. It was the thought of the boy that was giving him faith at last.

How could he let the rest of them know the boy wouldn't let them down? He would be back. He would bring help . . .

Morse code.

Could he remember it from the old days?

He lifted the bucket and began to tap out a tattoo of sound, a message.

Help coming back soon. Soon.

I plunged down and the ice cold of the water took my breath away. I kicked my legs out, heading straight forward, and then zoomed up to the surface for air, praying there would be a surface.

My face hit rock. Only enough space for my mouth to grab some air and pull it into my lungs. I trod water, using my hands to move myself along the rock, only my face above the water. I tried not to think of being trapped in there for ever. Dying in that dark chamber.

At least I could breathe. I was still alive.

One more minute of life is life. Where had I heard that? I couldn't remember but I held on to the thought. Stay alive for one more minute. At least it seemed that nothing was coming after me.

For a second I imagined that swishing sound moving swiftly towards me under the black water and I jerked my legs up involuntarily. Pushed the terrifying thought away immediately.

One more minute of life is life.

Surely a minute had passed and I was still alive.

It couldn't get any worse, could it?

The answer came a second later. I felt my legs being pulled by some kind of current. I tried to stay on the surface but the pull was too strong. I took one deep breath of air, and was sucked under.

32

They were sending someone at last. At least that was something. Bella Bartell still had some clout, some friends in high places. Hadn't she known this place was important from the beginning? But no one had listened. For so long now no one had listened to her – as if she really was a stupid old woman. But she had known what she was talking about.

Something was going on in this town. Now the tramp was gone, and the boy too – a boy, she told them, with no memory, and someone after him. A boy who needed help. And now, at last, someone had listened.

They would come. They would search. They would find them all, alive. She held on to that hope.

Ryan sat up in bed. He felt he had let Ramon down. He could never trust his dad again. He looked up at the poster of Darth Vader on his wall. His hero. What would Darth Vader have done?

He would have gone up with his light sabre and saved the day.

But Ryan had been grounded. There wasn't a lot he

could do tonight. So he would sit here in his bed, sit up all night if he had to, and wait for something to happen.

He had a strange feeling that it would.

Dead and gone, the Reaper thought. A threat no longer. He had watched him dive into the deep waters and he had slammed the gate down. The Guardians must not follow. They were too precious. He controlled them. They turned and moved slowly back down the tunnel.

The boy had tried to ruin his moment, his great moment. Had tried to snatch it from him. Now he was gone.

Dead and gone.

33

I was being turned and tossed. I had no control over my movements. All I could think of was holding my breath, staying alive. Just one more minute. Faster and faster I was being hurled down, caught in a racing current. But where was I heading?

Even in the second I thought it, I knew – knew where I was headed. Knew where I was going.

Dobie's Doom.

It began in these hills – these hollow hills, Catman had called them – and then came out for an exhilarating moment into the open air, freedom, before it plunged back down into darkness again.

One minute would be all I would have to break free, to get out. Could I? Had anyone before me?

One more minute of life is life. I was still alive. I was not going down without a fight, without trying.

I longed to suck in air. If I couldn't take a breath soon, I would drown. *One more minute. Keep that thought. Hold it, Ram.*

And suddenly I was above the water, propelled at lightning speed as if I was on a rollercoaster. But at least I had air to breathe. I had to find a way to stop. I could feel fresh air, feel it whisk by my face. I was heading for the open, for freedom – that was the thought that kept me alive in that minute. If I had to die, I would die in the open air. Any moment now.

The instant I saw the black clouds in the sky I began to grab for something to cling on to. I would only have a moment in that hillside stream, and then I would plunge straight down. Already I could picture that gaping black hole, hungry for me. The rocks beneath my back rattled my bones; branches were ripped from my grasp when I tried to hold them. I reached for grass, for ferns, for anything that grew that I could cling on to. But the grass slid through my hands; the ferns were pulled from their roots.

I would not go down into that black hole! I twisted myself round, made a claw of my fingers and with all the strength I had left I clung on to a branch overhanging the Doom. My flesh tore, but my fingers held fast. I felt the pull of the water, refusing to let me go. But I was just as determined. For a split second it seemed to loosen its grip, getting ready to suck me over the falls. I grabbed my chance, swung my legs to the side. I prayed I could hold on, terrified to let go. I tried to pull myself up.

And the branch began to loosen. I felt it being dragged from the earth. And I knew if I slipped now I would slip for ever. I would never regain a hold. I dug my free hand into the bank, but it sank into soft mud. Any moment now I would go down, hurtle down, plunge down to my doom.

No! I kicked out with all the force I could muster, and my foot held fast. I found rock. I pushed myself up, got a grip with another foot. That was when the branch broke free. I almost tumbled back into the foam, but my hands immediately found another hold: a bush, a clump of nettles. I thought of nothing but holding on, moving up and out of the crashing waters.

I was shaking.

I was going to make it.

One more minute of life is life.

I rolled on to firm ground.

I was alive.

34

I lay on the ground for as long as I dared, trying to breathe again, trying to stop myself from shaking, afraid to sit up – sure if I did the sky would fall, the earth would move. I'd lose it: consciousness, nerve, life. Everything. But I had to sit up. I had to go. Warn someone. I knew Catman was down there, in a place no one even knew existed. He was down there, and so were the others. The others that Bella had been so certain had gone missing.

It was Bella I would go to. She was the only one who would believe me. She would make someone do something.

And me? I would disappear into the shadows once again, out of the clutches of the Dark Man. But I couldn't let Catman rot in those deep, dark chambers.

I got to my feet. Only now did I feel the ice-cold waters soak through into my very bones. I needed warmth, dry clothes, a hot bath. I began to make my way unsteadily to Bella's house.

What time was it? Night. A dark heavy sky, still raining. Didn't know anything else. Time running out.

Time. Time. Time.

I heard someone shouting – looked all around, sure

they were close by. The voice was so clear. But the words were in my head. I closed my eyes and tried to concentrate, so I didn't lose them.

'Time's running out.'

Someone had said that to me. No. Someone had yelled that to me. And now, I was sure that someone had been my dad. Needing me. Panic in his voice. 'Time's running out. It's up to you.'

'What is up to me?' I shouted it into the night sky, the rain splashing against my face. Time was running out for what? What was up to me?

I was running down a dark tunnel, with that voice yelling behind me, 'Time's running out. Get out of here. It's up to you now.'

I tried desperately to see where I was running, or what I was running from. But the sliver of memory, like all the others, suddenly dissolved into nothing. A blackness came over my mind.

I sat down.

Why had anything been left up to me? I was useless.

35

I was exhausted by the time I reached Bella's house. I expected to see a light in one of the windows – some sign that she was there, waiting for me. But the house was in darkness. I stayed in the shadow of the trees for a while, my eyes searching the road, the garden, before I sprinted from my hiding place to her kitchen door.

It was unlocked, as usual. I pushed the door open and stepped inside. Almost immediately Mata and Hari were curling themselves round my ankles, looking for food. Hungry as always.

They were annoyed because I ignored them. I wanted to see if Bella was anywhere about. But the house, the bedrooms upstairs, the living room, were all empty. No sign of Bella.

I looked at the clock. It was late, almost ten. Where could she be at this time?

I finally gave in to the cats and fed them. For the first time I realised I was shivering with cold. My clothes clinging to me. I'd be good for nobody if I didn't get into some dry clothes, have a bath.

Bella's bathtub had a rusty ring round it, and the water that came out of the tap was tepid and brown. I didn't care. I needed a bath.

I lay for only a moment, all the time thinking about what I was going to do next. Wait for Bella; tell her what I had found. Leave her to do the rescuing.

Would anyone believe her?

No. Bella would make them believe her. She would annoy them till they had to do something to shut her up. She would be able to take them to the spot where that hatch was. I would show her.

Then I would leave. I would have done all I could.

I awoke with the sound of voices downstairs. I was on top of the bed, fully clothed, ready to leave at any moment. Mata and Hari were still cuddled up against me. I had changed into dry clothes, and I remembered at once how I had tried my best to stay awake and watch for Bella, but I couldn't do it. I must have fallen asleep.

I sat up, listening. Couldn't make out who she was speaking to or even what she was saying.

She was late home, was my first thought. Where had she been until now? Mysteries. Bella was full of them. I crept out of bed, stole silently to the door. It was a man's voice. Deep, rich; it reminded me of dark chocolate. Ryan's dad? What would he be doing here at this time of night?

I crept further down the stairs, one soft step at a time, wary of making any sound.

I couldn't make out what they were saying, those whispering, murmured voices in her living room. Whispering as if they were afraid someone might hear.

'I knew you'd come,' was all I could hear of Bella's voice.

And then, the man's voice, clearer now. A voice I knew.

'You know you've always been someone we trusted. I think we have to find that boy.'

I didn't have to see his face. His voice was enough.

False. Treacherous. Deadly.

The Dark Man was here.

36

How did I keep from yelling? From falling? My teeth began to chatter, and not from cold. The Dark Man had found me again. But how? How had he found me this time? There had been no reports of a missing boy, or even a dead one. No publicity. Yet, of all the towns in the world, he had come here – come to the place where I was.

Only one answer. Bella. She had let him know where I was. I thought of the emails I had seen her sending – furtive emails sent in the dead of night. Telling him where I was; telling him to come.

I had told her about the Dark Man and she had brought him here, feet away from me. I had to get away. Right now.

My hands were shaking as I reached for the door, praying it wouldn't squeak, praying they wouldn't hear me as I left.

I opened the door as silently as I was able. Opened it only a crack, gave myself just enough space to squeeze through. I was almost sure I would make it, until I felt my arm catch on something. I glanced back, hardly turning my head. My sleeve was caught on a man's coat laid along the hall table – a long, expensive, dark coat; dark like him. I watched with horror as the coat began to slide to the floor. The silk lining seemed to have a life of its own as it slid and slithered to the ground. I reached out to stop it but it was too late. The coat fell. Something tumbled from the pocket. A mobile phone. His phone. It seemed to me it crashed to the floor with a sound as loud as cymbals. They would hear. They had to hear.

'What was that?' The Dark Man was on his feet in an instant.

So was Bella. As quick as him despite her age. She was at the door ahead of him, pulling it open. She spotted his coat on the floor, and Hari, turning a guilty winking eye at her.

'Sorry. One of my cats.' She lifted the coat and hung it up on the hook on the wall. 'Sorry,' she said again. Then she opened the front door and let Hari out.

Catman sat on the cot, exhausted.

He had given up on life, but the boy never had. The boy had come for him. He would hold that thought, because it was the boy who was giving him hope. He had found this place and come to rescue him. Rescue the others. He would bring help back.

Now Catman wanted to live, wanted to be free. All those years he had thought only of death and then, when it had been so close, he had longed for life. He would go back, he decided, back to his family. He had run away and running away hadn't solved anything for him. Only made him more bitter. Well, he wouldn't run away again.

If he could just have the chance to get out of here.

He had to keep them all hoping.

He took up the bucket and began pounding on the walls again. *Help coming soon.* He beat out the rhythm again and again.

I crouched behind the hedge, hoping and praying they wouldn't come outside – wouldn't realise I'd been there in the house, so close. My fingers closed on the phone in my pocket. I couldn't resist snatching it up in that moment before running from the house. *His* phone, and who knew what secrets I might find in it? A clue to my past, to my identity. It was a mad thing to do really – instinct had taken over. I hoped he wouldn't check his pockets, not right away, and realise his phone wasn't there. Know someone must have taken it. I wanted to look at it right now, but I didn't dare. I was sure I was wheezing so loud with nerves they must hear me. I caught my breath as the front door opened. Felt as if I was stuck to the ground, sinking into the mud.

But it was only Hari who slunk out, then sat on the doorstep out of the rain.

The door closed.

I was safe, for now.

I began to move – the further away from the Dark Man the better – all the time trying to work out what I should do.

151

I could never trust Bella after this. Not after seeing her with the Dark Man. There had always been something suspicious about Bella. Even Ryan had figured that out. Right from the beginning he had said she wasn't the daft old lady she appeared to be.

Ryan.

If I couldn't trust Bella, Ryan was the only other person in the town I knew. And he was a boy, like me. I should have known never to trust an adult. Better sticking with people my own age. They had never let me down. They had always been the ones who helped me. Gaby and Zoe, and Faisal and Kirsten. And now, Ryan.

I needed someone to alert the authorities that there was something going on in that underground bunker. The missing people were hidden there. Catman too. They needed someone to rescue them.

I couldn't risk staying. The Dark Man was here. I had to run. Ryan would have to do it for me.

I smiled. In spite of everything – my terror of the Dark Man being so close – I smiled thinking of Ryan. He would be the one who would save everyone. His dream come true. Famous. The great detective.

I had to find Ryan, get him to help.

Then I would be away, away, like all the other times when the Dark Man almost had me. Well, he wouldn't get me this time either.

37

'Are you still awake, Ryan?!' It wasn't a question, Ryan thought, it was a complaint.

His mum barged into the room. 'Get into bed. Now!'

He had his pyjamas on, but underneath he was still wearing his outdoor clothes, his shirt and trousers. Why did parents never realise how important it was to be ready to spring into action at a moment's notice?

He lay in the dark after his mum had gone, but he couldn't sleep. He didn't dare sleep, listening for sounds in the night, watching the sky outside his window for any signs of strange lights.

He couldn't tell how long he had been lying there when something suddenly rattled against his window. Not the rain. Pebbles? He leapt from his bed, stood looking down into the garden. At first he could see no one, and then, out of the shadows, Ramon emerged from the bushes. He was safe! Ryan waved wildly at him, but Ramon didn't wave back. He only acknowledged Ryan with a nod and a furtive look up and down the garden, as if at any moment someone would appear and grab him. He beckoned him down.

How? Ryan wanted to ask. How was he going to get

out without his parents sussing it? But a detective would never ask a question like that. He'd find a way.

His parents were in the study as he tiptoed downstairs. His dad would probably be working on his presentation for that big promotion he was always talking about.

He pulled open the front door but hardly closed it behind him. Didn't want to be locked out. There was no sign of Ramon. He crept round the house stealthily, keeping close to the wall, scared to call out his name.

He almost let out a yell as he was grabbed and dragged into the bush growing against the side of the house. It scratched against his face. An arm was locked round his neck, a hand clasped over his mouth. For a moment he remembered one of his theories . . . that maybe Bella's grandson was an alien too.

'It's me, Ram – on.' He seemed to stutter over his own name. 'Don't yell.'

Ryan squirmed from his grasp, turned to face him. 'You gave me the fright of my life there. What's all the secrecy? Where have you been? I thought you'd been abducted by aliens.' Ramon seemed to think about that. 'Were you?' Ryan added fearfully.

'Of course not,' Ramon said. 'But I have found something and you have to help.'

This was getting more interesting by the second, Ryan thought. 'What did you find?' But Ramon seemed reluctant to go on. What was wrong with him? 'Are you OK?'

He shook his head furiously. 'No! I'm not OK.' He leant against the wall, put his hands over his face. 'I have so much to tell you, Ryan . . . I don't know where to start.'

'Tell me. Is there something I can do to help you?'

'You're the only one who can, Ryan.'

Ryan stood tall. The only one who could help. Wow! 'Tell me everything,' he said.

Ramon leant further against the wall of the house, backing so far no one could see either of them in the bushes. Ryan followed him.

'I'm not Bella's grandson.'

'I knew it!' It took all Ryan's control not to shout it out. 'She is an alien, isn't she? She kidnapped you, wanted to abduct you too.'

'Of course she's not an alien,' Ramon said. 'But I think she might be something much worse.'

'Wow!' Here was a mystery indeed – the kind he had been waiting for all his life.

'I'm going to tell you a story, Ryan, hardly believable, but it's true. My name isn't Ramon. I don't know what my name is. I have no memory. I woke up a few weeks ago in a tower block somewhere and since then I've been running. Someone's after me, someone's always after me. I call him the Dark Man. He's from my past. I don't know who he is. I don't know why he wants me.' Ramon tapped his head angrily. 'I've got some terrible secret locked in here and he wants to find out what it is! Then he's going to kill me.'

For a moment, Ryan was sure Ramon was going to cry. He hoped he wouldn't do that. He didn't. He just stared at the ground for a moment, then he sniffed and went on with his story.

155

'The night I came here, I saw something strange up in the valley. I tried to run away and fell, knocked myself unconscious. When I came to, Bella was standing over me. I thought then she'd rescued me; now . . . I think maybe she was part of it. She brought the Dark Man here.'

'He's here? In the town?' Already this Dark Man had become real to Ryan. His dark shadow became substance. Ryan could picture him waiting, ready to leap at them, leap at Ramon.

'He's here. So I have to move on. I have to run. Right now. But there's more, Ryan.'

How can there be more? Ryan was thinking. *How can anything be more exciting than this? A boy with no memory, a hidden secret, the Dark Man.*

'You were right. People have gone missing. And I've discovered where they're all being kept.' Ramon pointed beyond the town into the darkness. 'The hills are hollow, Ryan. Inside there is . . . some kind of underground bunker.'

An underground bunker? Ryan had read about them, built to house government officials if there was a nuclear war. But one of them here?

'But if it's not aliens, who is doing this? Who is . . . and why?'

Ramon was shaking his head. 'I don't know. It might have something to do with Bella. I don't understand everything. All I know is I can't go back there. I have to move on. It's all going to be up to you, Ryan. You can do something. Get the police to go up there. I'll tell you exactly where to go.'

But Ryan was way ahead of him. 'I know where to go. I thought they had taken you. I followed your footprints up into the valley and then . . . they suddenly just disappeared. As if you'd been lifted up into the sky.'

Ramon beamed at him. 'There's some kind of hatch. It's hidden, but it's there. Just where my footprints disappeared. You can climb down. There's something down there.' He didn't seem to want to go on, but he did. 'Tell the police to be careful. There's something weird down there.'

Weird. Nothing was going to convince Ryan aliens weren't involved in this somewhere.

'You can have that place investigated.' Ramon said. 'You! You'll be the great detective. The hero. And I can just disappear again.'

Ryan was already picturing it. His name in the paper, interviews on television, the beginning of a great career. 'But that wouldn't be fair, Ramon . . . you're the one who found it, not me.'

'Don't care, Ryan. I just have to get away. You don't know how afraid I am of the Dark Man. I have to stay out of his clutches till my memory comes back. But I want Catman and the others saved. You can do that for me.'

'You can rely on me, Ramon,' Ryan said.

Ramon smiled. 'And my name isn't Ramon, by the way . . . I haven't a clue what my real name is, but I call myself Ram.'

38

Dead. Dead in the water. At least he was supposed to be. But the boy had survived. What was it about this boy? He would be such a good specimen. Now it was vital that he get him back – after all, the boy knew where they were all kept. He had to get him, keep him, one for his collection – but how? First he had to find him. Had he left the town already?

The Reaper dismissed that. No. Somehow he didn't think the boy had left the town. Too much of a hero. He would want to save everyone. No one else had ever found the place – so secret that even the government had forgotten about it. It had never even been used. They had built it, but underestimated the power and proximity of Dobie's Doom, cracking the walls, pounding them down. They had even blasted a hole in it before it was abandoned, thinking it would flood, be lost for ever.

But it hadn't flooded, not completely. And he, the Reaper, had taken it over, adapted it with cells and even gates for the Guardians. He had always been good mechanically, even when he was a boy, trapping animals in cages he had built himself. Keeping them for his collection. He had always collected things. But this was the best collection he had ever had.

Yes, everyone had forgotten about this bunker.

But the Reaper hadn't. He had always known of the place. Knew that one day, the right day, Judgement Day, the bunker would be useful.

And now . . . that day was drawing closer.

The boy would be his prime specimen. And if he couldn't find the boy . . . who knew? Perhaps the boy would find him.

I waited in the garden shed for Ryan. He was going to bring me food for the journey. I could see how excited he was about what I had told him. More excited about my secret past than about what was in the bunker underneath the hills. Had I done the right thing confiding in him? I still wasn't sure, but I had to tell someone. Someone had to investigate those bunkers, find out their secret.

I couldn't tell Bella. I didn't trust her any more. Maybe I never had. Bella, who had rescued me, taken care of me, nursed me, but had too many secrets herself. She knew the Dark Man.

At that moment, I remembered his phone. There in my pocket. I took it out, flipped it open, and it lit up with a green light. The shed seemed to be filled with it. I punched the address-book button, but nothing came up. His address book was empty. Neither was there any record of calls made or received. He must have deleted them all. Maybe he had even changed phones, discarding one and using another. What had I expected? The Dark Man was a smart guy. There was nothing here to help me. I had risked taking the phone for nothing.

Ryan was shaking as he opened the fridge door. His mum was in bed, but his dad was still in his study at the back of the house. Why did everything make a noise when you didn't want it to? He'd already stepped on a squeaky floorboard he didn't even know they had. Now it seemed to him that the fridge door creaked. He held his breath, listened, waiting for his dad to suddenly appear and ask what he was up to. He had his story already rehearsed. *Midnight snack, Dad. I'm a growing boy*. Wasn't his mum always telling him he didn't eat enough?

He lifted cheese and a packet of corned beef along with an unopened tray of tomatoes. Enough for Ramon . . . no . . . Ram . . . Where did he get that name?

Maybe, he thought, Ram would need some more warm clothes. It was March, ice cold outside and still raining. He looked around for something he could give him. Up in his room he had woollen sweaters; surely his mother wouldn't miss a couple of them, at least not for a while. And an old anorak too.

Ryan listened at the door before tiptoeing back up to his room. He left the food in a plastic bag on the hall table. It would only take minutes, no, not even minutes to bound upstairs, lift the sweaters and be back down here. His father was busy. He could hear him on the phone. He would be in that study for ages. He always was, working till all hours.

Mum would say, 'I just hope it's worth it.'

'Better life for our son – that's all I care about,' his dad would answer.

For a second, even as he hurried upstairs to get the clothes, Ryan felt warm all over thinking about his dad. That was all he ever cared about: making the world a better place for his son. He'd do anything for his dad, he thought. Poor Ram. He didn't have anyone who cared about him.

He tiptoed back downstairs. And almost fell down the last few steps.

There, standing at the bottom of the stairs, was his dad, holding the tomatoes in one hand, the cheese in the other. He looked up at Ryan. Ryan tried hard not to look guilty, felt his face go red, his cheeks flush.

'So, what's all this, young man?'

39

Ryan was trying to think up a good story. He was hungry, wanted a midnight feast in his room, but carrying a couple of sweaters and an anorak as well? How could he explain that?

Anyway, wasn't he going to tell his dad about the underground bunker when Ram was clear and away? What difference would it really make if he told him now?

It was too much for one boy to handle on his own.

'You know Bella's grandson?' His dad nodded. 'Well, he's not. I told you there was something fishy going on and there is. Bella's not his grandmother. He's on the run. She picked him up the other night, up in the valley.'

His dad's face looked as if he didn't believe him. 'Is this another of your stories, Ryan?'

Ryan shook his head. 'No, Dad, you have to believe me. He needs to get away. There's someone after him. Some man . . . the Dark Man.' The words tumbled from him. 'He's lost his memory. He's hiding out in the shed. I was bringing him food. Dad, we have to help him. Please.'

Bella realised the boy had been back. His wet clothes were still on the floor of the bathroom, a brown rim around the bath itself. Course, she never cleaned the bath anyway, but no – this was definitely a fresh brown rim. The boy had been back. He had been in the house while she was here, and he had sneaked away. Why? Where had he gone? And why had he left?

She should tell the man about this, she thought. She should phone him and tell him the boy had been back.

I waited in the dark of the shed. My heart was thumping as I tried to think out my next move. How to get out of this town without the Dark Man ever knowing I was here. I thought of our last encounter and I smiled. Yes, I had fooled him that time. Only metres away from him and he still couldn't find me. Maybe I was cleverer than I gave myself credit for.

Don't speak too soon, I thought. I still had to keep out of his clutches.

The door suddenly creaked open. I moved back, let the mobile phone slip back into my pocket, careful not to be seen. But it was only Ryan.

'Come on,' he said.

I stood up, moved towards him just as another shadow filled the doorway.

I gasped with horror: a dark shadow, a man's shadow. Ryan must have seen my fear. He reached out to me.

163

'Don't worry. It's only my dad. He's going to help you get away.'

I was annoyed at Ryan. 'You shouldn't have told anyone. I warned you.'

'It's my dad. He's going to help you. He'll get you away, and then he'll take the police to the bunker in the valley. I don't know what your problem is.' Then Ryan explained to his dad, 'He's worried about anyone else knowing. He has to get away, hasn't he, Dad?'

His dad stepped into the shed, touched my arm. 'You come into the house. We'll get everything sorted.'

I was led reluctantly into Ryan's house, into their brightly lit hall and then their living room – clean, warm, inviting. The kind of home I dreamt of . . . and yet I still wanted to run.

Ryan's dad looked at me. 'You wait in here.'

'What are you going to do?' I asked. 'You're not going to tell the police about me, are you?' I glared at Ryan when I said that.

'No. I realise you just need to get away. What if I took you away from here . . . drove you to the next town? You can get a bus, a train somewhere. I'll give you some money.'

I was already shaking my head. 'No. Thanks, but no. You need to take the police to save those people. Ryan can take you to the exact place.' It seemed so long ago I had been in the bunker that it all seemed like a dream. Yet it had only been a couple of hours maybe. 'Just let me go.'

'Wait here.' He smiled at me – deep blue eyes, like Ryan's. 'I can't just let you go without some kind of help.

I'll sort things out. But I promise I won't tell the police about you, Ramon.'

Could I trust him? I was champing at the bit to be away. Just wanted to disappear into the night.

'His name's not Ramon, Dad. It's Ram.'

His dad, heading out of the room, turned quickly, looked surprised. 'Ram?'

Ryan explained to him. 'I told you he's lost his memory. He doesn't know what his real name is, but he calls himself Ram.'

Ryan's dad bent down to speak to me. He stared into my eyes. 'From now on, you are not going to be alone in this. You need help. I'm going to help you. OK?'

Ryan stood proudly behind him. His dad was doing exactly what he wanted him to do. I wasn't so sure.

Ryan kept looking at me and smiling, wanting me to feel reassured.

'Can I stay here with him?' he asked his dad.

'No, Ryan, we have a busy night ahead. Go to your room and get changed. Put on warm clothes.' He turned back to me. 'Do you need anything? Are you hungry, thirsty?'

Finally, they both left. Left me alone.

Or was I alone any more? What stopped me from running then? Because for the very first time in ages I didn't feel alone. Someone was going to help me. Ryan's dad. Surrounded by a family, the Dark Man would never get me. Maybe Ryan's dad knew a psychiatrist who would probe into my brain and unlock my memory and the secret I had in there. I sat back on the sofa and closed my eyes. It wouldn't hurt surely to wait a few minutes longer. I hadn't realised how tired I was. If only I could let myself sleep.

It was at that very moment the phone in my pocket began to rumble. The Dark Man's phone. My hand was shaking as I lifted it.

Someone was phoning the Dark Man. The number was local.

Bella.

It had to be Bella. I had to hear her, hear what she had to say to him. I flipped it open.

But it wasn't Bella on the phone.

'I've got him,' the voice said.

It was Ryan's dad.

40

Ryan's dad and the Dark Man. But how? The phone fell from my shaking hand. I heard Ryan's dad ask warily, 'Hello? Are you there?', knowing something was wrong. I had to get away. But where, and how?

Ryan's dad knew who I was, the boy on the run, the one the Dark Man had been searching for . . . and now, he had betrayed me. But how was he connected to the Dark Man?

And Ryan?

No. Ryan would know nothing about it. He had told his dad for the best of reasons. To help me.

Maybe now, he would have to help me again. I was out of here.

I made for the door, pulled it open and there, blocking my way, a dark shadow, was Ryan's dad. My breath caught in my throat like something solid. I stared at him. He stared back. 'Going somewhere?'

I tried to make my voice sound normal. 'Need some fresh air. I was just going outside.' He didn't know I had the phone, couldn't know I had heard him . . . Could he?

'Better stay inside.' His bulk moved me back without touching me.

'I really think I need that fresh air,' I insisted.

But I knew he wasn't going to let me out of there. I glanced at the window. Tight shut against the cold night air and the rain. He followed my glance, took his eyes off me for a second and I was past him. 'I think I'm going to faint,' I said, hoping he would just let me go, believe me. But the mobile phone was lying on the sofa where I had dropped it. He couldn't miss seeing that now. He was after me in a second, anger in his movements. I ran for the front door, and suddenly, Ryan's mother was there, hurrying from another room.

'Help!' I shouted to her. She looked puzzled, glancing from me to her husband.

'Get him!' he snapped at her. 'He's the one we've been looking for.'

And those words almost made me faint. Ryan's mother! She was one of them too. I sidestepped her, darting into the dining room and from there into the kitchen. Surely I could get out the back door. I reached for the handle, and a knife as big as a saw came whizzing past my hand and embedded itself in the wooden door. I jerked back and almost fell, looked round. Ryan's mother had thrown it. I glanced this way and that, trying to find a way out. And there was my escape: steps leading from the kitchen to an upstairs landing. I was on them in an instant, leaping from the floor to that first step. Ryan's dad threw himself at me. A couple of centimetres and he would have had my ankle, but he only banged his hand on the step. I was up them three at a time, slamming my way through the door. Ryan was up there. They surely wouldn't hurt me if I was with Ryan.

I called out his name as I ran. 'Ryan!'

Ryan couldn't understand why his dad had made him go to his room at this important time. He'd said he was going to tell Ryan's mum about Ram, even when Ryan reminded him it was supposed to be a big secret.

Oh well, he thought. He could trust his mum, couldn't he? She would want to help Ram too. But why make him stay in his room? It was so unfair.

'When we need to know where the bunker is I'll come and get you. Until then, I don't want you involved,' his dad had said. But he was already involved. He was Ram's friend. He had promised to help him.

He had heard his dad on the phone, making arrangements – about Ram probably – but it was the crashing sound from the living room that finally decided him. He couldn't sit there any longer. Then he heard footsteps banging on the stairs. Something had happened to Ram. He leapt to his feet. He didn't often disobey his dad, but this was a special occasion, he decided. He couldn't just sit there and do nothing.

And suddenly he heard his name being called. 'Ryan!' A scream. A cry for help. Ryan was out of the door in an instant. Ram was running towards him. There was terror in his eyes.

'Help me!'

And his dad – he was running right behind Ram. Ram stopped for a second and it was just enough time for Ryan's dad to grab him roughly by the arm.

Ram's eyes never left Ryan's. 'You have to help me,

Ryan. Your dad's in with the Dark Man . . . Help me!'

'Back to your room, Ryan.'

He had never heard his dad talk to him like this before. 'But, Dad,' he said.

'BACK TO YOUR ROOM!'

Ram was struggling wildly. 'Ryan, help me!'

Ryan didn't know what to do. He looked at his dad, wanting him to explain. He wanted to run to Ram, help him. But he was so mixed up, confused, frightened. 'Dad!' He was screaming now too.

Ram broke free, pulled himself away. It was only Ryan blocking his way that held him back. His dad grabbed Ram again, held him roughly by one arm. This time he swung him round, lifted his hand and brought it down right across Ram's face with a force that stunned Ryan to silence.

Ram slumped to the floor.

Ryan was crying. 'Dad. You've killed him, Dad.'

'Get in your room, Ryan.'

But Ryan couldn't move. He watched his dad lift Ram's limp body over his shoulder and carry him back downstairs.

41

Dr Mulvey was at the door. 'I saw your light, Bella. Are you all right? How is the boy?'

She thought about letting him in, was about to open the door wide. In fact, he almost took a step inside. Then she changed her mind and stood in front of him. No good telling anyone, even Ben Mulvey, too much. 'He's gone home,' she lied. 'I've just been working on my computer.'

Ben screwed up his face. The old fool didn't believe her, of course. 'That boy's been through a lot over the last few days, Bella. You should have kept him here.'

'He wanted home to his mum. She's been missing him.' Already she was picturing the scene. The boy sleeping peacefully in his own bed, this imaginary mother mopping his fevered brow.

'And what about you, Bella? You seem to have so much on your mind. Is there anything I can do to help?'

Oh, she so much wanted to tell him everything, everything she knew, at least. Have this burden lifted from her. But she said nothing. She only smiled.

Dr Mulvey moved away from the door reluctantly. 'You know my number if you need me.'

Bella watched him go down the path and get into his car. She closed the front door.

She didn't want company. She had too much to think about. Could she be wrong?

She had almost phoned the man who had been there, thought carefully about it. She even had the phone in her hand, and, all at once, she had felt that shiver in the back of her neck. That shiver that had never let her down in the old days.

It was then she had started thinking of all the boy had told her. His nightmare vision of the Dark Man coming for him. The Dark Man who so terrified him.

The Dark Man . . . and she had thought of the man who had come to her house. She had sent for him. They had never listened to her before, until this time, when she had mentioned the boy. And he had come – a tall, dark man . . .

No, it couldn't be . . . She tried to dismiss it.

But what if it *was* him? She had told this Dark Man all about the boy. Had the boy seen him here? She imagined that he had. Imagined him listening to them, thinking he had been betrayed. Betrayed by Bella Bartell. She, who had never betrayed anyone in her life, even under torture.

Poor little mite. Had she placed him in even more danger?

And he was in danger, she was sure of it. If only she knew where he was.

Ryan sat on his bed. He was shaking all over. He had

expected his mother to come up and tell him what was going on, but she hadn't appeared. He waited for his dad, trying desperately to think of a rational explanation for why he would hit Ram. Hit him so hard he might have killed him. He couldn't bear the thought of his dad going to prison. Would he lie for him? Tell the police he had seen nothing? Was his dad going to ask him to do that?

He's in with the Dark Man, Ram had said.

But that was nonsense. His dad didn't know any dark man. Yet, even as he thought it, he remembered his dad's friend, the man who came now and then in the black car, who would disappear into the study with Dad while they discussed business.

The Dark Man?

No. There had to be a rational explanation. His dad would have one. Maybe Ram had gone crazy and his dad had only been trying to calm him down. Maybe Ram was crazy, like daft Lenny – making up all these stories about lost memory, and secrets and underground bunkers.

The door of his bedroom opened. His dad stood there, his face grim. Ryan didn't say a word. Couldn't. He had so many questions to ask and yet he couldn't open him mouth to speak.

His dad came towards him, sat on the bed beside him, took his hand. 'I'm going to tell you something, Ryan. Something that's going to change your life.'

42

She couldn't wait any longer. She was going to find the boy. She had thought about sending another message, but who could she trust?

She grabbed her coat. Mata was up at the window, calling for food. 'You've had enough,' Bella told her. That cat would eat anything.

Bella tightened her coat about her, took the gun from the drawer. She was going to find him. And there was only one person she could think of who might be able to help her. If he didn't trust Bella, then there was only one other person he would go to.

Ryan, the boy detective.

Maybe they were going to be Miss Marple and Sherlock Holmes after all . . .

Lenny was at the door waiting for her, his big face covered with a grin. All teeth. He was the last person she needed to see.

'I have to go out, Lenny,' she said slowly.

He nodded. 'Can I come in? I'm hungry.'

He was as bad as her cats, she thought. 'I'm going out,' she said again.

'Won't be any bother,' Lenny said. 'I'll feed the cats.'

Bella shuddered. The last time he had fed the cats he had eaten half of their food himself. 'Tuna,' he had explained. 'It said so on the can.'

'I don't know when I'll be back, Lenny. It's late. You go home.'

Lenny looked up at the sky. 'Bad things happening tonight. They're coming back. Soon.'

'Yes, I know, Lenny.' She patted his arm. 'But you'll be safe this time.'

She waited till Lenny had lumbered back along the path and started off down the street. Only then did she turn and lock her door, something she never normally did. Then she moved softly, but not on to the street. Her plan was to cut through the bushes and trees, taking the back route to the house next door. She didn't want to be seen.

She looked back only once. And Lenny was still there at the end of the street, watching her. He was caught in the glow of the street light and there was an expression on his face she had never seen before. A look that made her shiver.

A look full of sinister intent.

43

I came to in the cellar, with just a narrow bead of light shining through the bottom of the door at the top of the stairs. It took a moment for my eyes to become accustomed to the dark. How much time had passed? My face ached with pain. I felt my jaw, certain it was broken. I was sure I was about to vomit.

It took me another moment to piece together all that had happened. Ryan's dad's blow still made my head spin. Ryan's dad, one of them. One of who? But he was in it with the Dark Man . . . and his mum too. What was going on? This was a family, a nice ordinary suburban family.

And Bella too? How many people were part of this conspiracy?

I imagined the Dark Man heading for me, coming closer. If only there was a way for me to get away from here. My only hope was Ryan. The hope that he would come down and let me out. I stood up and my head felt as if that bell was back again, clanging ever louder. What if he didn't come? What if he couldn't? Maybe his dad would lock him in his room till I was safely away

Safe – that was a joke, a horrible joke on me. For I

knew I would not be safe. The Dark Man was coming and when he had me in his clutches . . . I felt sick again at the thought of what he might do to me to find out what I knew . . . But what *did* I know?

Help yourself, Ram, a voice whispered. *You have no one else*.

No. I wouldn't give up. There must be something down here in this musty cellar that would help me. There was a narrow window at ceiling height, shuttered with wooden panels and locked tight. I pushed at it but it wouldn't budge. Even if it had opened, it was so narrow there wasn't much chance of being able to squeeze through.

I fumbled around in the dark. Boxes. Boxes and cartons and black bags. A long thin torch. I switched it on and in its beam I saw tools neatly held on the wall – a hammer, a chisel. Would I be bold enough to use them? I thought again of the Dark Man and I knew I would. It took a lot of strength to pull the hammer from the rack, but it finally came. I held it in my hand, weighing it, thinking of how when the Dark Man came down those stairs, I would be hiding behind them. I saw myself swinging the hammer hard against his ankles, bringing him down, giving me a moment to leap up and out of the cellar. Ryan's dad would be behind him, ready to catch me, hold me. My mind was in a turmoil of plans, and still my head throbbed with pain. All I wanted to do was sit in a corner and sleep. But if I didn't come up with a plan to get out of here, I would be sleeping for ever.

Help me, somebody, I prayed silently, knowing there was no one. No one I could rely on.

Gallacher had called him on the back-up phone he kept in the car. He had told him that the boy was with him, trapped. He had him. He had him at last. This time there would be no mistakes. He had been on his way back to Bella's house to find his phone, thinking it had only dropped from his pocket. And the boy had taken it. He had been in the house with him, and hadn't known it. The boy was clever, resourceful, but the phone would have been no help to him. He would have found nothing on it.

He nearly smiled as he drove past Bella Bartell's house. She had led him here, found him for them. Good old Bella . . . Lucky it had been him who had taken her call. Everyone else was fed up listening to her. Now he would find out the truth, and then the boy would be gone for ever. For good. And just in time.

Gone for ever.

The Dark Man liked the sound of that.

The hammer fitted snugly into the waistband of my trousers, ready for use. I began to look for something else I could use, still trying to figure out what link Ryan's dad had to the Dark Man. They were in this together, whatever 'this' was. And whoever 'they' were. Why was I so important? They didn't want me dead. Certainly not yet, not until the Dark Man had me. What was it about me that made them so afraid?

I pulled at one of the boxes and an envelope full of old

photographs fell on to the floor. I gasped at the sound, hoping it wouldn't send anyone down here to investigate. They were photographs of Ryan and his family. Ordinary everyday family photographs. They scattered on to the floor and I shone the torch over them. There was his mother, waving, riding a bike – they were abroad somewhere. She was wearing shorts and a wide-brimmed straw hat. In another, Ryan and his dad out fishing, holding a trout between them, grinning like idiots. *These can't be bad people*, I thought, *not with a son like Ryan, not fishing and riding bikes and laughing. Surely not?* Yet I was here; I was trapped. My head still reeled from the blow Ryan's dad had struck.

It was the Dark Man's face that made me notice the last photograph, or else I would have kicked them aside. But I couldn't miss that dark face. Those dark, menacing eyes. In the photo he was standing straight and tall. Handsome even. Not smiling. Did the man never smile? Ryan's dad was with him. *He* was smiling. There were three of them in the photograph; three soldiers dressed in desert combat gear. The Dark Man, Ryan's dad and another man in the middle of them. His face seemed familiar but I didn't have time to study it. For at that instant I could hear something moving outside the house. I stuffed the photo deep into my pocket.

In the dark of the cellar all I could make out was the narrow window leading to the garden. Now it was being forced open. Someone was out there.

44

I pulled the hammer from my waistband and held it high, ready to bring it down if this was an enemy.

'Boy, are you in there?'

The voice took me by surprise. It was Bella's. The shuttered window was pushed wide. Her face appeared. She was lying on the ground, peering through at me.

'What . . . what are you doing here?' I stumbled over the words.

'I came to sell perfume. What do you think I'm here for? To save your neck, of course. Can you squeeze out of here?'

The opening was so narrow I was sure I wouldn't even get my head through. But I tried. I shoved the hammer back into my waistband and stood on the boxes. I did my best to squeeze myself through, but it was impossible.

'Come on, you're not trying hard enough,' she said.

I felt like shouting at her that I would have cut my head off if it would have helped me escape, but try as hard as I could, my head wouldn't fit through that narrow opening.

Bella's voice became soft. 'Your Dark Man's here. He's in the house. I saw him driving past me. As soon as I saw him stopping here, I knew they had got you. Lucky I was in the shadows or he might have seen me. He'll be down any minute.' There was a heartbeat's pause, then she said, 'Now, can you get your head through?'

I had never moved so fast. My face scraped against the woodwork, my ears jammed against stone, but the thought of him so close, maybe even now taking one step at a time heading down to this cellar, made me desperate. All at once I had a head made of rubber. It bent, it folded and at last, I was through – my head, then my shoulders, and I was out into the pouring rain. Bella hauled me to my feet.

'Come on. No time to waste. They'll be after you now.'

'How did you know I was in the cellar?'

'It was a lucky guess. My house is the same as theirs. I've got a cellar just like that one. If I was going to hide someone, that's where they would go. OK?' She didn't pause as she spoke, pulling at me, darting in between the bushes. And she didn't stop talking, her words spilling out of her. 'It's my fault he's here. Your Dark Man. I called him. Told him all about you.'

I stumbled, afraid. Another betrayal? Was she going to suddenly push me ahead and there he would be, waiting for me in the trees? I couldn't handle that.

Bella gripped my hand tight. 'I'm sorry about that. I didn't know who he was . . . They've never listened to me before. All my suspicions and no one ever listened. Until I mentioned you . . . a runaway boy with no memory, and suddenly, he arrives.'

'But who is he? And who are you?'

She turned for a second, smiled, but didn't pause in a single step. 'I wasn't always a daft old woman. I used to be a daft young woman. I used to be a spy.' She said it so casually I wasn't sure I had heard her properly. Then I remembered the photographs I had seen: Bella in a uniform, Bella receiving a medal. How stupid of me. She'd been getting a medal for bravery, no doubt. And the gun . . . now I understood.

I had judged her as a daft old woman and she was anything but.

'Ryan's mother and father are in on it.' I said that and didn't even know what 'it' was.

'Sleeper cell,' she muttered.

I didn't know what that was either. It was as if she knew I wouldn't understand. 'Ordinary family doing ordinary things, till the time comes and they leap into action.' Her quick steps faltered for a moment. 'There must be something big coming . . . really big. If there's one sleeper cell, there must be more.'

'Ryan doesn't know anything about it.'

She paused. 'Maybe not,' she said.

We were heading beyond her house, out into the darkness.

'Where are we going?' I asked breathlessly.

'Anywhere away from here,' she muttered.

The Dark Man burst into the cellar, switched on the light. 'He's not here.'

Gallacher was down the stairs before him. 'He has to be. He's hiding.'

He followed him, pulling over tables and boxes. It was clear in a second the boy had gone. 'Is there a way out?'

Gallacher pushed open the narrow window. 'It was locked tight. It's always locked tight. Too narrow for him to get out.'

The Dark Man studied it angrily. 'Opened from the outside . . . by someone who knows how.'

'Someone's helping him?' Gallacher said.

'You idiot,' the Dark Man said. 'You can never under-estimate that boy's ability to make friends. Bartell. They say she was the best in the old days.'

Bella and I headed down the overgrown path between her house and the Gallachers'. She moved so stealthily, so silently, I was impressed.

'Why did you retire?' I asked her.

She didn't even turn. 'Didn't want to. They thought I was too old.' She kept hurrying on, not losing her stride. 'Soon as I came I knew something was wrong here, but they wouldn't listen. They thought I was trying to get back in, making up mysteries. But I knew I was right. I thought it all had to do with the people going missing. I was wrong about that. It's to do with you and the secret you've got locked in that head of yours. You have to get away. The missing people are something entirely sepa-rate. I should have been more careful of Lenny . . . I think he has something to do with them.'

I suddenly remembered Catman. I pulled her back. 'Bella, I know where the missing people are. I know where Catman is.'

Her face went white. 'We have to get them, save them.' She slapped her head. 'So much to do. But first you have to get away. I'll get Catman and the others.'

Bella – a spy. Hard to believe looking at her now. But she had saved me, hadn't she? Saved me from the Dark Man. I believed in her.

She turned to move on, and suddenly, our way was blocked. Someone had stepped from the trees and was standing in front of us.

It was Ryan.

45

'Ryan, thank goodness it's you,' I said. 'You've got to help us.'

Bella seemed to stiffen beside me. I held her arm. 'It's OK, Bella. Ryan knows. He'll help us.'

'I came here to think,' Ryan said, and I saw then how pale his face was, streaked with tears. 'My dad's been telling me a lot of things.'

'Don't listen to him,' Bella snapped. I tightened my grip on her arm. *Don't antagonise him* – I sent out the silent message to her. Ryan loved his dad. I could understand how mixed up he must be feeling.

'I know it's all hard to figure out, Ryan, but I'm a good guy, remember? You're always on the side of the good guys.'

'Dad says he's a good guy.'

'You saw what he did to me.' I could still feel the power of that blow. 'Good guys don't do that.'

He drew in his breath, looked from me to Bella. 'Why should I trust you? Or her? I've always been able to trust my dad.'

'Because I'm your friend, Ryan. You've got to help me get away, then you're the one who's going to rescue those people in the bunker, remember? They're relying on you.'

'My dad says they're nothing to do with us. He says they're . . .' He searched around his mind for the word. '. . . expendable.'

'Expendable!' Bella snapped it out angrily. 'That should show you once and for all that your dad is no good guy.'

Ryan stiffened when she said that. How I wished she would shut up.

'Your dad didn't mean that. He was just angry, angry at me.'

'He said you were dangerous.'

'How could I be dangerous? I'm just a boy.'

Bella sniffed. 'We're wasting time here. We're moving on.'

Ryan looked at her, stared at her. I could almost read his mind. He didn't like Bella, didn't trust her. Why should he choose her instead of his dad? Why should he choose me?

'Ryan,' I said softly, 'you want to be a detective, don't you? On the side of law and order? Well, now's your chance. Let us pass. Don't tell anyone you saw us. That's all we're asking, Ryan. You don't have to help us . . . just let us pass.'

At last, Bella picked up on my tone. Her voice was quiet, gentle. 'Yes, son. You don't have to do anything to help us. Just let us pass. And say nothing.'

He was almost there, I was sure. I could see he was thinking hard about it, trying to do the right thing. He was a good boy, Ryan. Suddenly I could hear voices in

186

the distance. His dad, the Dark Man. They had found me gone. They were already after me. 'Please, Ryan,' I said. 'Listen to how close they are. Please don't give us away.'

Bella backed me up. Her voice was soft. 'Yes, Ryan. You're a good boy. You were always a good boy.' The men's voices grew closer. Sounds whispering through the trees. She nodded in their direction. 'You could never be one of them.'

Ryan stood up straight when she said that. His eyes glittered in the darkness – seemed to harden to steel.

And I saw then he was lost to us. Because whatever his father had told him had made him want to be 'one of them' more than anything else. His voice suddenly bellowed into the night air. 'They're here! Dad! I've got them. They're here!'

Then he turned that steely gaze on Bella. 'I *am* on the side of law and order. But we're going to be the new law and order soon.'

46

I made a run at Ryan. Taken by surprise he was knocked off his feet. Still he grabbed my sleeve, holding me back from running. Bella pulled at his arm, smacked his hand. It must have hurt, for Ryan yelped and loosened his grip just long enough for me to move.

'Come on,' Bella urged me. 'You have to get away.'

I could hear the calls behind me – Ryan's dad, the Dark Man too, coming closer. The hunt was on. Bella dragged me through the bushes.

I lost sight of Ryan, already on his feet, hatred for me in his eyes. Where was the boy I had got to know, the friend I thought I had? Where had he gone?

He was an enemy now.

Couldn't think about that. Had to concentrate on saving myself. Me and Bella. She was plunging ahead. I couldn't think where we were going, somewhere through these woods. I had to rely on Bella.

'They're getting closer.' She was right, I could hear them. Bella turned to me. 'You have to get away. Keep out of their hands.'

'Not without you,' I said.

'Oh, come on, don't be a hero. They won't hurt

me. But . . . if they get you, it's all over, don't you see that?'

'I can't leave you. I don't know where to go.'

'You've stayed alive all this time. You can stay alive for a while more.'

Their voices ever closer, the rustling of bushes too close. She pushed me. 'Go on. You go one way, I'll go the other, lead them away from you. That's all that matters.'

'What do I know, Bella?'

'I don't know, but they're a part of it. A sleeper cell. Something big must be planned. You can stop it.'

'Will I see you again?'

She grinned that daft grin of hers. 'Too right. I'll make the front pages. Old Bella saves the day.'

'The missing people . . . you'll make sure they're saved? You'll find them?'

'Thinking of them at a time like this? You are a good boy. No wonder someone trusted you.' I wanted to hug her and there wasn't time. 'Thanks, son,' she said. 'You made me feel useful again.'

Then she pushed me so hard I stumbled against a tree. 'Go!' she barked, and she was off down another path, branches crackling behind her. Gone.

I heard her call, 'Come on, son. Run!' as if she was calling to me, urging me on. As if I was running beside her.

I was off, seconds after her, picking my way stealthily, trying to make as little noise as possible. I could hear them following after Bella, turning away from me.

'Please, God,' I prayed. 'Let her be OK.'

Ryan was sent back to his room and he wasn't happy about it. He wanted to run with his dad, take up the chase with him. Instead, he was banished back to his room. It wasn't fair. He had found them after all. He wanted to go after Ram, wanted to find the old woman. He was angry at her. Angry that she should have implied that he was not made of the same stuff as his dad. His dad had explained it all to him, and now he understood. He had known all his life that he was different, that he was special. Now he knew why.

And people like Bella Bartell didn't count. Expendable, his dad had said. He understood exactly what his dad had meant. Too many people were expendable. Not necessary.

Like Ram. He was needed now – his dad had explained that. But soon he too would be expendable.

He had hated going back to the house. Hated not being part of what was happening. But he must obey orders, his dad had told him. So he slunk back to his room and sat on the bed. He didn't even put on the light. He wanted to sit in the dark, and think.

He stared into the darkness, and who did he see?

His poster of Darth Vader, dressed all in black, standing menacingly against his enemies.

Now he knew why Darth Vader had always been his hero. He had gone over to the Dark Side.

And now Ryan had joined him. And he liked it.

There was nowhere else for her to run. They were catching up. At least they had both followed her, not the boy. *So, let them find me*, Bella thought. By now the boy was far enough away, surely, to be safe. She couldn't run much longer anyway. Her breath was coming in short gasps. *Too old for this kind of thing, Bella old girl*, she was thinking.

'There she is! Get her!' They must have seen her through the trees, stumbling to a halt.

She called out, as if urging the boy on. 'Run on ahead. Get away, boy. Leave me.'

Hoped they would believe her.

She waited till they were almost upon her before she finally stopped. Couldn't have run any further if she'd tried.

She was bent double, catching her breath, when she heard a familiar click. She knew it from old. Hadn't heard it for so long.

The click of a gun.

She turned slowly. It was Ryan's dad. That nice polite man who had come to her door . . . Had that been only yesterday? Respectable, well-mannered, hiding a terrible secret.

Now he held a gun.

'Where's the boy?' His voice was hard.

'Long gone,' she whispered. 'Too smart for you lot.'

She saw the anger flush his face. 'Where is he?' he asked again.

And this time he took a step forward, gun raised,

pointed straight at her.

She brought up one hand to point towards the town, as if that was where the boy had gone. She pointed to distract him from her other hand, moving slowly to her pocket, where her own gun lay heavily against her side.

But he spotted her movements, was taking no chances.

Did she see the bullet as it sped towards her? She was sure she did, as if in slow motion she could make out the silver streak of death, hurtling in her direction.

She, who had lived through so much, helping people escape from East Berlin, finding out secrets that had saved so many lives, risking her own almost daily and, now, dying almost outside her own front door. *It would be funny*, she thought, *if it wasn't so tragic*.

Dr Mulvey didn't stand a chance after all.

The Grim Reaper had got to her first.

Get away, *boy*, she thought. *Don't let them get you.*

Then she thought nothing else at all.

47

I heard the shot. Had to be a shot. It stopped me in my tracks. Bella. I wanted to shout out, run towards that sound. Surely they hadn't shot Bella? She was an old woman. They couldn't have killed her. No. I wouldn't believe it. The shot had been meant to warn her, make her stop. Ryan's dad wouldn't kill an old lady.

But then I remembered the blow he'd struck me. My face still ached with pain. He'd had no qualms about knocking a boy unconscious – what would stop him shooting an old woman?

And Bella wasn't just any old woman. She had known all along something was going on in this town. What had she called it? A sleeper cell. Bella had been a spy in her younger days. Not any old lady – a smart old lady. And I knew in that moment that Bella was dead. Too dangerous to them to let her live. I leant against a tree, exhausted and afraid. My one friend. The only one I could really trust any more. Gone.

Alone again.

But Bella had wanted me to live. She had pushed me away from her, led them away from me. 'Stay alive. You have to.' For her sake, for Bella's sake, I was going to do just that.

The Dark Man was not pleased that Bella was dead. He stood up from her limp body and glared at Gallacher. 'You shouldn't have killed her. She could have told us things.'

'She had a gun,' Gallacher said. 'I thought she was going to shoot. I wasn't taking any chances.'

The Dark Man's eyes accused him. 'Too late to think of it now. We have to get her body hidden. Can't leave it here.'

'You go after the boy,' Gallacher said. 'I'll take her back.' He nodded at Bella with no compassion in his eyes at all. 'I'll put her in my cellar till we can dispose of her. Another victim of Dobie's Doom.'

The Dark Man imagined the boy peering at him through the branches of the trees, laughing at him, sure he would never be caught, that he bore a charmed life.

He and Gallacher had known each other for many years. Friends, associates, comrades. Surely together they could flush out one young boy. And now, he was sure that boy must know more than he pretended to.

He called himself Ram.

More dangerous than ever.

Without a word, the Dark Man ran on into the woods.

As I ran, I thought about what to do next. Where could

I go? The Dark Man would be close behind me. Where would he expect me to go next? As far away from this town as possible. How could I fool him?

I'd beaten him before. I would again. Kept out of his clutches, always a step ahead. I wasn't going to be caught, not now. If I had time to stop, think, put things together, all I'd learnt, I could work it out.

Sleeper cell.

The photo in my pocket.

'We'll be the new law and order soon.'

But there was no time to stop, a luxury that might cost me my life. I had to keep on running. Nothing else mattered.

But something did. A voice inside reminded me.

The people in the bunker. Catman. I stopped dead then, remembering them. Who would save them if I didn't? Not Ryan. They were expendable, he'd said.

Not Bella. Bella was dead now.

My throat hurt thinking about her.

I was the only one who knew about the bunker, knew there was a secret hidden in there. If I ran now, no one would ever find them. I thought in horror of being left deep underground for ever.

No. Couldn't do it.

You can't have been a bad person, Ram, I told myself. Because I couldn't leave without doing my best to save them.

A phone call. An anonymous phone call to the police.

But would they believe me? So many calls about alien visitors. The police, Bella had told me, filed these cases away, ignored them. And anyway, how could I explain where the bunker was. I would have to take someone there, show them the exact spot where the hatch was. Ryan had known because he had found my footprints.

I'd been running so fast, so caught up with my thoughts, that I was out of the woods on the common behind the town. A house lay before me, lit up still with Christmas lights. On the roof, a beaming Santa on his sleigh. The doctor's house.

Bella trusted him. She even fancied him. I would go to the doctor; I could take him and show him where the bunker was. The police would believe the doctor.

I began to run again. Yes. I'd tell Dr Mulvey about the underground bunker.

48

I saw a hint of fire through the glass. The doctor still up. No need to rouse him then. I was astounded that it was still night, still dark. I felt as if days had passed since I'd escaped from the bunker and been tossed down Dobie's Doom, not hours. I peered through the window. No sign of anyone, just the gas fire crackling in the hearth as if it was real, giving out a warm welcoming flame, and a single lamp by the fireside chair. The room was filled with warmth and comfort. I should feel guilty breaking into an old man's bedtime. Then I remembered Bella, the bunker, the missing people, Catman – and knew I had no choice.

He came shuffling into the room from his kitchen, munching on a sandwich, dropping crumbs as he walked. His glasses were perched on top of his head. I watched him fumble round the table, searching for them. I rapped on the window.

At first he didn't hear. He put down his sandwich, patted the pockets of his trousers, still looking for his glasses. I rapped again, louder this time – and now he looked up, looked towards his front door, as if the sound came from there.

I almost cracked the glass when I knocked again. And this time his eyes darted to the window. He started back when he saw me, as if he'd just seen a ghost. A ghost at the window. I waved my arms wildly, mouthed to him, '*Let me in!*'

He moved slowly towards me, still trying to take it in. I could almost read his thoughts. Was I real? Was he imagining things?

'What . . . what are you doing here?'

He fumbled with the window catch. Finally, he pulled it inwards. I was on the sill in a second. A moment later I dropped on to the floor.

'Close the window. Shut the blinds.' I was doing it as I spoke. 'You have to help me, Dr Mulvey.'

He looked agitated, and I wondered why I had asked this daft old codger to help me. But I had no one else. I needed someone to rescue the people in the bunker, and most of all I needed to get away from here. I pulled at his arm. 'Dr Mulvey, Bella's dead. She's been shot. There are people after me.'

He blinked, couldn't take in what I was telling him. I could see only confusion in his face.

'Bella . . . dead? How?'

'Yes. Dead. Shot. And the people who shot her are after me too.'

This time it was him who pulled me, towards the fire, as if he needed to see my face in the glow to make sure it was me. 'Are you making this up? Shot?' He felt how wet my clothes were. 'You're soaked through. Sit by the fire. And look at your face. Who did that to you?'

My hand automatically went up to my face. I could

feel how swollen it was already.

'That doesn't matter,' I said. 'I think I know where the missing people are. You have to take the police to them.'

'Who's missing? What are you talking about?'

I knew I wasn't making any sense, but where to start in such a story? 'The people Bella said were going missing . . . Catman. The others she was always talking about. I know where they are.'

His head seemed to clear. 'You know where they are?' he repeated. 'Sit down, son. Tell me. First I'm going to get you a blanket.'

It seemed an age before he came back, was probably only minutes. He shuffled back and wrapped a warm cream blanket round my shoulders.

'There's no one gone missing,' he said. 'Bella was always on about that –'

I interrupted him. 'No. She was right. I know where they are. You've got to help them.'

He looked puzzled, unsure of whether I was making all this up.

'I think Lenny might have something to do with it,' I said.

His eyes almost popped out of their sockets. 'Oh no, never Lenny! The boy's simple.'

I was shaking my head. Bella thought Lenny had something to do with it, and I was going to believe Bella. 'Maybe he's not so much simple . . . as mad,' I said. 'But he's big and strong . . . strong enough to carry the people down there . . .'

'Down where?'

I held up my hand. I would tell him that later. 'Maybe

199

he has some warped idea that he can keep them for when the aliens come back, so they'll take them instead of him.'

The doctor spoke as if to himself. 'He *is* terrified of them coming back.'

'I know . . . and if he's crazy he'll think he's not doing anything bad . . . maybe he doesn't even mean to hurt them. Please say you'll help, doctor.'

'Tell me everything,' the doctor said.

Where had the boy gone now? Leading him one way then another. So close, always so close, but never close enough. The Dark Man turned quickly as he heard the rustle of trees behind him. He melted into the undergrowth.

It was Gallacher. 'You have to come back to the house. Ryan thinks he knows where we'll find him.'

49

The doctor sat across from me. He hadn't taken his eyes off me once, listening with a look that grew more and more incredulous with every word. I couldn't blame him. My story was a tumble of words. So much had happened, so much to tell. I just hoped I was making some kind of sense.

He stood up when I'd finished. 'I'm going to phone the police,' he said. 'It's them you should be telling all this to.'

I was on my feet in a second. 'I can't wait around for the police. I can't talk to them – that's why I came to you.' My eyes kept darting to the window, as if at any moment the Dark Man would come leaping through.

The doctor was shaking his head. 'What is your mystery, son?'

I wished I could tell him. 'I don't know. But I feel I'm close to finding out, close to something. All I do know is that I have to keep as far away from this Dark Man as I can.' I tapped my head. 'I have something in here he needs to find out. I just don't know what it is.' It sounded so crazy, so unbelievable. But Bella was dead, and that seemed to be all the proof he needed to help me.

He came over to me, patted my arm. 'I don't understand any of this, but you're obviously afraid.' He paused. 'Go then. I'll alert the police, though heaven knows how I'm going to explain all this.'

'I can't go yet. I have to show you exactly where this place is. You'll never find it otherwise.'

'I hadn't thought of that,' he said. 'OK . . . You take me to the place. I'll have my mobile, so I can contact the police from there. How would that do?'

'That's perfect . . . but please, let's hurry.'

I imagined the Dark Man close outside, going from place to place, searching for me.

'I'll get my coat.' He turned away, then suddenly swung back. 'Ah! Hold on. At least I can give you some food for the journey.' He disappeared into the kitchen, moving faster than I'd ever seen him. Good, he would need to be alert to convince the police. I was only eager now to get away. Couldn't stand still. He came back a moment later, carrying a mug and a bag of fruit and biscuits.

'Here, hot soup. You need something warm inside you.' I only realised then how hungry I was. Nothing to eat, since when? I couldn't remember. Everything merged into a blur. I took the mug from him, warmed my hands around it.

He was already pulling on a long woollen cardigan. He left the room to get his coat, and I began to drink the soup. It tasted awful. It must have been made by Bella. I expected to see her red hairs swimming in it.

Bella! Tears rolled down my face thinking about her. Poor Bella.

'I would have to take you there,' Ryan was trying to convince them. 'I wouldn't be able to tell you where it is, but I can show you.' He had said it so many times he was beginning to believe it himself. It would be so much better if he could take them there himself. He didn't want to be left out of anything after this. This night – everything he had learnt – had indeed changed his life.

His dad looked concerned. Ryan didn't want to let him down. It seemed important to his dad to stay on the right side of this Dark Man.

No wonder Ram had been afraid of him. Ryan felt the stirrings of fear of him too, even here, in his own bedroom, with his dad standing right beside him. This was the first time he had seen him up close, here, in his own room. Seen the length of him, the menacing dark violet of his eyes.

And his dad? It was clear to Ryan who was in charge. No. He couldn't let his dad down.

'I can take you there,' he said again.

The doctor was ready. Raincoat, hat, even a scarf wrapped round his neck. He lifted his car keys from a dish on the hall table and took the mug from me. 'Shall we go?'

For the first time in so long I felt a release of tension. Someone was going to help me. But I couldn't relax. I had to keep my adrenalin up and running. Till I was safe.

Well, *safer* at least.

'Now, you slide in the back seat, lie on the floor. If anyone sees me out at this time, they'll just assume I'm on a call.'

The car was parked close to the doctor's front door. I slipped silently inside, slid on to the floor. A moment later the doctor was in the driver's seat and the engine was turned on. 'I'll get you out of here,' he said softly.

Lenny saw it all. Standing in the shadows, watching. The boy was in the car. Did he really think he hadn't been seen?

Lenny smiled. He knew where they were going. He would use the shortcut, get there before them.

It was time.

50

When the road became dark and we began to move into the countryside, the doctor told me I could sit up on the seat. It was safe now, he said, away from the houses. Sitting there, watching the branches of the barren trees zoom past, my eyes began to close. I wanted to sleep. Couldn't sleep. Too soon I would be out of the car, and had to be ready to run again. I watched the doctor's eyes in the mirror, watching the road, flicking back to me.

'Sleep if you wish,' he said.

I shook my head.

'A few minutes won't do any harm. Winston Churchill swore by those little slices of death.'

I kept blinking to stay awake. The last thing I wanted was a slice of death.

'I'm so glad you're doing this, doctor. I told Ryan about the missing people too . . . but he won't do anything now . . . They're expendable, he said.' I couldn't bear to think about Ryan. 'No one's expendable . . . are they? Everyone is useful for something.'

'My thoughts entirely,' the doctor said. I looked up at him. And it looked like two faces in the mirror, blurring and blending into one. Was I hallucinating because of lack of sleep . . . ?

Then I dopily realised we were fast-approaching a bend in the road where we needed to turn off and head up a dirt track into the valley. But before I could get the words out, he was already making the turn.

A cold weight settled in my stomach and my head spun as my brain sluggishly came to the awful realisation. 'You don't need directions . . . do you, doctor?'

His eyes smiled at me in the mirror.

Bella had thought it was Lenny behind the abductions. But she'd been wrong. It was the shaky old man who'd come to visit me that first day. Didn't look so shaky now. Firm hands gripped the wheel, and the eyes that looked back at me were sharp and cold.

I tried to open the car door, but my hands were like jelly – wouldn't do anything I wanted. 'What was in the . . . ?'

I didn't need to finish the question. 'The soup?' he said. 'Oh, nothing that won't wear off.' The doctor looked over his shoulder at me, and suddenly he wasn't Dr Mulvey any more. His eyes seemed wild and unreal. I didn't know this man, didn't recognise him at all. The car came to a halt.

My mouth was so dry. But I wanted to know, had to ask. Finally, the words came thick and slow. 'Who . . . are . . . you . . . ?'

His eyes went wide. His voice was strange, unearthly. 'I am the Reaper.'

Lenny was waiting – already there, eager to help. The Reaper needed Lenny. Lenny was strong. He could carry his specimens down into the bunker. Lenny could carry them alone, flung over his back. His only reward, all he wanted, was protection from them. The ones who had taken him before. If Lenny obeyed his rules he would never have to go back, the Reaper had promised him.

A promise easily made and easily kept. Lenny, a specimen? As if the gods in their chariots would accept him. Those supreme beings, who since the Incas, the Aztecs, the Ancient Egyptians, had been visiting earth, shaping human civilisations, choosing only the best to take back with them. And he, the Reaper, had gathered a collection of fine specimens for them to study.

Hadn't they thrown Lenny back the first time? Of course they had. No. The specimens he had harvested would be most gratefully received and he, the Reaper, would become one of them. One of the gods. It had been written in the stars.

He had been told in the stars he must become a doctor. Doctors were trusted, allowed into people's houses, allowed to give them injections, drugs, make them docile, unconscious – all that was needed so that Lenny could bring them down here. A few of their things packed in a case, a handy cover story, and no one suspected a thing.

Lenny hauled open the back door of the car and stared at the crumpled body on the seat. 'Is he dead?'

'Of course not . . . I do not kill. But he's been prepared for deliverance. He will make a good addition.'

The Reaper opened the boot of the car. He took out the green gowns, the masks. They were on the gods' business and had to be dressed appropriately.

Once properly garbed, Lenny lifted the boy out easily, swung him over his shoulder as if he was a sleeping bag. The boy almost had it right. That was the reason he was so dangerous. But it was not Lenny who was the mastermind – as if it could be Lenny!

'Yes, he has a brain this one. I'm sure the gods will be very happy to study it.'

51

My head banging off steel – cracking, painful, like explosions in my skull – was snapping me awake. I tried to open my eyes. Blackness all around me. I could smell dank water, rust, sweat. I was back in the bunker. My eyelids felt as if they had weights on them. I was being carried over someone's shoulder. Whose?

I wanted to sleep again. Couldn't. Wouldn't dare. I had to stay awake. My life depended on it. The doctor, Dr Mulvey, was he carrying me? No. Way too old. And he was weak. Bella had fancied him. I had trusted him. We'd both been wrong.

My last sight of him had been in the car mirror, his eyes gleaming with evil – mad eyes, watching for me to pass out.

I bit my bottom lip hard to keep from passing out again. I tasted blood. I would not let drowsiness overtake me. *Think, Ram.*

Luckily, I had only taken a few sips of the awful tomato soup – it had reminded me too much of Bella. I had chucked the rest in one of the doctor's plant pots. Thank goodness. It must have been powerful stuff.

The shoulders carrying me easily were broad and strong.

Lenny.

I opened my eyes again, and now the corridor was lit by a strange green glow.

'In here.' It was Dr Mulvey's voice, yet not his voice. No longer kind and gentle, but menacing and cold and, somehow, not human. As if it was coming through some kind of microphone.

I had a feeling that 'in here', wherever that was, was the worst place I could go. Once there, how would I ever get out? Trapped, like the rest of the people down here.

I looked along the corridor, a tunnel of steel. Bulbs on the roof were giving out that gloomy green light stretching into darkness.

I, too, would be locked in steel.

No.

I could outrun both of them if I had to, drugged or not.

My life depended on it.

The Dark Man spotted the car, parked where Ryan had led them.

'It's old Dr Mulvey's,' Ryan said.

'I thought no one knew of this place.'

Ryan shrugged.

Had the boy run to this doctor for help? He always could find friends no matter where he went. Had he moved on and left this doctor to save his missing people? Anger surged through him. If he were only to find an old doctor in here who knew nothing of the boy's whereabouts, then . . . No! That would not happen. Not like the boy at all. Always the hero. The doctor was old, weak. He would need help. The boy was here. He was sure of it.

Ram. He called himself Ram. Proof, if he had needed it, that the boy knew more than he pretended.

He called to Ryan, 'How do we get in?'

Lenny swung me from his shoulders to his arms, so that I was lying on my back. I lay limp, pretending I was still out cold. I almost gave myself away when, through narrowed eyes, I saw that the doctor was wearing a mask. A strange, alien-looking mask and some kind of green gown. I tried not to stiffen with fear. Here were my weird figures. I watched the doctor's hands grip a lever, one of several set in rows on a panel fixed to the side of the tunnel. The wall beside him began to slide open. So that was how the cells were opened. And once in, there was no escape. This was to be my prison. No way was I going in there.

I shot my legs out as hard as I could, taking them both by surprise. I hit the doctor's mask and blood spurted out of the nostrils. The doctor fell back against the wall, clutching at his face. I heard him yell out, crumple to the ground with a splash as he hit the wet floor.

Lenny was strong, but slow. When the doctor stumbled, he dropped me. He bent down to help the doctor. I rolled from his grasp, and then I was up and on my feet and running. Lenny reached for the doctor's hand. I heard him shout, 'Stupid! Get after that boy!'

But by that time I was well away down the corridor. How could I let Catman and the rest know I was back? No handy metal bar now. And with a yelp of joy I remembered the hammer, still tucked tight into my waistband. I pulled it out, and as I ran I banged at the walls furiously. I wanted them all to know help was here. Someone was here. I was back.

And I wasn't leaving here until every one of them was free.

52

The Reaper got to his feet, the doctor no longer – angry at the stupid lump who was Lenny. Always too slow, and now . . . the boy gone from his grasp.

'Go after him!' He yelled it out again.

Lenny still held on to him, hauling him up, holding him as if he was too old, too unstable to stand alone. He threw him off, stronger now. He could feel the change inside him. The change he always felt when he thought of what he was meant to do, the future he was meant to create. The change that turned him into the Reaper.

'Go after him,' he ordered again, and this time Lenny obeyed. He turned and began to lumber down the corridor.

The Reaper even managed a smile. What was he worried about? The boy was trapped. There was no way out from here. Now he knew what waited out there, he would not take his chances with the water again. Only by some miracle had he survived last time. No, the Reaper thought. They would get him back one way or another. And, as a last resort, if he had to, he would unleash the Guardians.

Catman ran to the door. He had heard the resounding crash against the wall. Someone was there. Help at last? He searched around in the dark for the tin bucket. He had to let his rescuer, if there was one, know he was alive. He was ready. They were all ready. *Just get me out of this place!* he thought, and banged the bucket against the wall. The sound seemed to reverberate around his cell, and outside into . . . whatever was out there. He waited . . . then banged again, tin against steel. Morse code. *SOS*. *Help*. And then, another sound came back. An echo? No. They were all listening. They had all been waiting, just like him. He heard an answering SOS. *Get us out of here!*

I hammered against the walls as I ran, hearing at last the answering sounds. People coming alive – defiant, eager to be free.

'Help on the way!' I shouted it, even though I knew they could not hear my voice. Here in the bowels of hell, help was on its way to them.

But how, with Lenny closing in behind me? Any second I expected him to turn the corner, throw himself at me. I wouldn't stand a chance against him. I had to find a way to give myself the edge. I stopped dead, looked up at the roof. For the first time I could see the long worm-like pipes that ran along the ceiling. There was space between them and the roof. A hiding place. I could easily squeeze between the pipes, but surely the burly

Lenny would never be able to follow, or even have the sense to think I might be hiding up there.

I could hear his footsteps splashing nearer. No time to think about it. I threw myself up at the pipes. First time, my hands slipped through the slime. Desperation makes you inventive. I scrabbled at the wall, found a foothold, grabbed at the nearest pipe. Slime wasn't going to stop me now. Lenny's footsteps were seconds away.

I gripped the pipe tight, hauled myself up and squeezed between them.

Ryan had taken them to the spot where the footprints had disappeared. Bushes and grass kept the entrance hidden, camouflaging the hatch, but the Dark Man soon uncovered it. Now they all stood looking at it.

The boy was down there. The Dark Man could always sense when he was close. Who was he trying to save? Why should he care for people who didn't matter? And when had he turned into some kind of hero?

No time to speculate about all that. He had a picture of the boy slipping through his fingers again, and something like panic gripped him. The Dark Man couldn't let that happen, wouldn't let that happen. Not this time.

53

Catman was on his feet, strength roaring back into him. He thought of the boy, had thought of him all the time he was in here. After all the boy had come through, he hadn't given up, he'd never given up.

Was it the boy out there, come to save them? He imagined him running along the corridors, beating on the doors, alerting them all, bringing them hope. Now he needed them to do something for themselves. But what? He felt all around the walls. There was no escape from this cell. Only the door somewhere on this wall – a locked steel door with no handle. He banged at the walls, kicked at them, swung himself up and ran at them.

He knew it couldn't really be the boy . . . could it? But the thought of him made Catman eager to fight, so he clung on to it. He lifted the bucket again and banged it furiously, as if it might cut through the steel like a scythe through grass . . . He yelled at the top of his lungs, 'I'll find a way out. I'll help . . .' *If only*, he thought, *that could be true*.

I was on the pipes, lying flat, still as death. Directly

above Lenny. He had lumbered softly up the corridor, and came to a halt below me, almost as if he knew I was close. The green light gave his hideous mask an unnatural glow. I thought for a moment about dropping on top of him. Bringing him down. Knocking him unconscious. Taking him so much by surprise he would fall to the ground.

In my dreams.

Half boy, half robot, I might have managed it. Eighty per cent boy, twenty per cent gorilla, no bother. If I had special powers or gadgets I could use to floor him, I'd be down there in a flash.

But I had nothing. Only me. If I could just find a way to get those people out, maybe I would have some help. Maybe there would be a chance.

I held my breath as Lenny seemed to tense, listening. I listened too. Did I hear footsteps in the bunker? Someone else here, apart from the doctor? But the banging in the cells took over again and I heard nothing.

Why had I come back here when by now I could have been miles away? Free. Safe, for a while at least, from the Dark Man.

Then I remembered Catman and the others locked in here for eternity if I hadn't come back. No one knowing about them; no one to help. A living hell. And I didn't ask myself that question any more.

A drip of slimy water dropped from the pipe. I watched it fall almost in slow motion, gleaming like an emerald. It landed on Lenny's head. He smacked his brow, and then, slowly, as if he was just now remembering that there were pipes above him, he looked up. I could see his eyes through the mask. They scanned the roof, the pipes. I hoped he would be too dumb to imagine I could be hiding here. For a moment I thought he was. He tilted his head, first one way, then another, while I lay hardly daring to breathe. I could almost picture the slow wheels in his head creaking into life. Then his eyes went wide and, with a speed that made me jump, he threw himself up, grabbed at the pipe, began to haul himself towards me. He would never get through, I told myself. Never. But I wasn't taking any chances.

I moved. I have never moved so fast. Tumbling, rolling along the pipes. I heard his laboured breathing and knew he had made it, forced his body through the pipes, and was even now close behind me. In horror I realised I was heading back the way I'd come – too late to do anything about it now. For a split second I dared to glance over my shoulder. And there he was, loping, bent double, crawling like some dark alien creature, his eyes intent on getting me. I wanted to remind him how I'd helped him, how I'd stuck up for him. But this was no longer the Lenny I knew. This was like something out of a nightmare. I turned my eyes away, tried to forget what I had seen in his, and raced on.

54

Catman was crazy with energy now, kicking at the walls, aching to be free, hearing the others just as wild as he was. He wanted to burst through the door. He wanted out.

The Reaper listened. They were all going mad. It was the boy's fault. All the boy's fault. He held a handkerchief to his mouth, filled with blood. The boy had kicked the mask against his face, and the device that disguised his voice had broken his teeth. He hated the boy in that moment. He had known he was dangerous right from that first night when he had seen him in the valley. He should have taken him before now. But the boy would not get away again. If Lenny didn't catch him, he still had one last ploy to trap him, and he would use it.

I had to keep ahead of Lenny. My feet kept slipping on the slime of the pipes, but I couldn't let that slow me down. I was desperate. Lenny still behind me, ever closer. This was a different Lenny. Not the half-witted giant, but a creature urged on by blind obedience to his master – the Reaper – determined to bring me back to him, like a prize. The Reaper. And I was heading back his way. Had no choice. My mind was thinking as fast as I moved, thinking of ways to escape, get away. But how?

I could see through the narrow gap in the pipes on to the ground. Cells below me, sounds echoing around me. Cells with doors. He had been planning to put me inside one of those cells, open one of those doors. Something clicked in my head: the Reaper, standing with his hand on a lever, watching the door slide open.

And if he could slide open one door with a lever, I could open them all that way. The thought made me move even faster. I knew where I was going now, back to that panel of levers. I just had to make sure I got there before Lenny got me.

55

Here at last I saw it, bathed in green light: the cell at the end of the corridor, where they would have put me had I let them. The door still gaped open, waiting for me. No sign of the Reaper now. My eyes searched around for the levers, found them. I had one hope of beating Lenny, still hurtling towards me. I was young, slim, able to slip through the gap in the pipes that he would struggle to squeeze through.

But before I had time to position myself for the drop, Lenny's great paw shot out and caught my foot. I let out a yell, and with my other foot kicked against his masked face. I knew I had hurt him but still it didn't make him let me go. He only gripped tighter. This time, with both feet I made a scissor action, hitting his face and head as fast and as hard as I could. Lenny felt it. He let out a painful moan, but never loosened his grip.

I struggled to pull myself free of him. But he was too big, too strong. I could never beat him. I had no strength to beat him.

And then I remembered I had another weapon, a weapon I hated using. But I would have to.

I drew in a deep breath and I let it out in a tribal roar.

221

I roared loud and long, like some ancient warrior going into battle. My roar became even louder as it echoed down the tunnels. Lenny's eyes went wide. The sound scared him. He couldn't stand it. My roar became a scream, and this time when I kicked out he let me go, clamping his hands around his ears. Still I roared, and the sound made me brave. I was scaring him and filling myself with rage. I roared. The roar gave me courage. Lenny fell back, shaking his head, holding his hands over his ears. I had no sympathy for him, not now. I was away from him in a second, slipping, sliding between the slimy pipes, dropping away from him. And still I roared.

Catman was on the camp bed, trying to push at the roof, looking for some edge to freedom in the dark. Were they all doing the same, he wondered, in all these cells? Clawing for freedom because someone out there had come and given them hope, was risking everything to save them?

He kept thinking of the boy – but it wouldn't be him. He was too young.

Yet it was his face he kept seeing when he pictured their rescuer. His small frame outside that door – hiding, running, fighting. He needed help. If only he could find a way out of this cell!

And it happened, his prayer answered in an instant. The wall was slowly sliding open. Catman leapt from the bed. He ran to the door, placed the battered bucket in the opening as a wedge in case it should dare to close again.

But it didn't close. It opened wider. First his hand went through, then his arm, and finally his whole body squeezed through. And all the while he screamed and he yelled and he roared. He was free!

Suddenly the hatch began to open. The Dark Man didn't know how – he and Gallacher had been searching the grass nearby for some form of control panel or lever, and found nothing. It didn't matter now. Eerie green light spilled out of the hatch and lit up the sky like a beacon.

The Dark Man turned to Gallacher and smiled. 'Let's get down there.'

The boy, Ryan, took a step closer, stood beside them. The Dark Man looked at him and shook his head. His father said, 'Get back to the car, Ryan.'

The boy's face froze. 'That's not fair. I told you where to find him. I want to come.'

'This could be dangerous,' his father said. 'Get back to the car.' The voice would not be argued with. Still the boy stood there, kicking at the earth.

For a second the Dark Man was sure he would argue, but after a few seconds' pause, Ryan turned and headed for the car, his shoulders slumped.

The Dark Man turned back to the hatch.

Gallacher said, 'Strange lights in the night sky. No wonder Ryan was sure there were spaceships. They were coming from down here all the time!'

But the Dark Man was more interested in what was below. There was a steel ladder leading down to dark oily water. 'An underground bunker? Here? Why didn't we know about this?'

Gallacher shook his head. 'We can't know everything,' he said. Then he suddenly cocked his head, listening. A sound echoed up from below. Was it voices or the wind? 'I hear something.'

The Dark Man swung himself on to the ladder. 'No time. Come on, he won't escape this time.'

56

I watched them all stumbling out. A girl, her hair wild, her dress torn – she was crying and looking all around her. She seemed terrified to step outside, looking this way and that, as if some even more terrible danger might be waiting for her. A man, too, almost falling to the ground – till the girl grabbed his arm and held him up. And then I saw Catman, and I yelled again. I had thought he would be weak, would have lost hope. But he didn't stumble or fall. He came out like a lion ready to pounce. He turned as I shouted his name, and his face beamed a wide smile. 'Everybody out!' I called to him. And he nodded.

I ran towards him, sure that Lenny was still up in the pipes, too terrified to move now that there were even more shouts and yells. 'The opening's this way. We have to get out. I have to get out.'

I pulled at his arm.

'You could have got away. You came back for us.' He squeezed my arm.

There were so many of them, walking like zombies in the green light, stumbling and trembling.

I yelled, ran in front of them with Catman at my

heels. 'This way,' I shouted. 'This way out!'

And they followed me.

The Dark Man saw him at last, heading down the long corridor, leading the people like some diminutive Pied Piper. Leading them out to freedom. He had him now and he began to run. He called to Gallacher, 'He's there!'

I saw him as he ran towards me and there was nowhere for me to go. I would have to pass him to make the hatch. No way. He would have me before I could get up the ladder and out into the open air. He was down here. I had known he would be. Ryan had led him here. I looked at Catman. 'Get them out . . . I have to go.'

He grabbed my arm, saw the Dark Man down the tunnel, heading towards us. He stood in front of me as if he would protect me, but I pushed him away. 'Get everybody out, please . . .'

And I turned and ran.

They were going crazy. The boy had let them all out, every last one of them. What was he going to tell the gods now? He had failed them, and they did not suffer failure. He hated that boy. Always had hated him. Now, he would get him. He had one last chance to finish him off.

The Reaper hurried to the cell where the Guardians were kept. He lifted the lever. The door slowly slid open. The Guardians were free.

57

The Dark Man saw him weaving backwards through the crowd of stumbling disorientated people, trying to merge among them, hide himself. He kept his eyes fixed on the small figure. The boy was going back down the corridor. No choice now. He knew his destiny was behind him. Where was he running to? Was there another way out? He doubted it, and yet you could never be certain with this boy. He knew Gallacher was at his heels, just behind him. Two of them, two grown men: a match for any boy. He moved faster, pushing people out of his way.

A woman grabbed at his arms. Middle aged, grubby, a strong smell of stale sweat oozing from her. 'Where do we go? Where are we?' She was looking at him for help, but in a fraction of a second she saw there was no help in his eyes. Her own gaze moved from him to the others shuffling ahead of her, and she moved off, following them.

The Dark Man turned back to Gallacher. 'Come on.'

Why had I come this way? Why did I always do the

wrong thing? Perhaps I could have got out through the hatch, pushing my way out first, been lost in the confusion. But no, he had been there, heading towards me. I had avoided him before – *there must be a way to keep ahead of him now*, I thought. Another way out. But this was an underground bunker. There would be only one way out. No other hatch. No other handy door. No portal into another world. *Take me into another world*, I prayed as I ran. But there was none. I was stuck with this world.

No, my only chance was to find somewhere to hide, evade the Dark Man down here until I could make my way back – back to that steel ladder – and climb to freedom.

The sounds of the people were diminishing. I could still hear screams and cries of fear, but way back in the green gloom. Where was Lenny? I wondered. Up there somewhere? My eyes automatically scanned the ceiling, the pipes, half expecting to see him staring down at me, ready to leap on me. I even pressed myself back against the wall, just in case he did.

And in a moment of silence, I heard it. That same swish of something terrifying somewhere up ahead of me. Coming closer.

I tried to think what it might be. My worst nightmare, I had thought the first time I'd heard it. But now, my worst nightmare was behind me. The Dark Man, heading my way, would have me if I didn't keep out of his grasp.

But something was there and it was coming closer.

Something dark and sinister . . .

I stood still, not knowing which way to go. Certainly

not back. And now, not ahead. I looked around me. Another corridor loomed to my left.

I began to hurry. Now the sound seemed to fill the metal tunnel . . . something lumbering, menacing, moving closer.

I almost crashed into the wall. The corridor was a dead end.

Dead end. Didn't like the sound of that one bit. There was nowhere else for me to run. And whatever was after me was only a corner away.

Turning.

At last I saw them.

Two of them crawling towards me, glittering green.

Alligators.

I suddenly knew what had happened to Lenny's fingers.

58

Ryan got out of the car, couldn't believe what he was seeing: people emerging out of the ground, looking all around them, puzzled, breathing in air, turning their faces up to the driving rain and the sky. He stood watching them, waiting for his dad, for the Dark Man to emerge too. But it wasn't his dad who climbed out of the hatch. It was Catman. He stood looking around, making sure everyone was there.

Where was Ram? Where was his dad?

A man came stumbling down the rocky path towards him. His eyes seemed wild, his clothes unkempt. He looked afraid. He reached out his hand to Ryan, like some zombie in a movie, and Ryan stepped back.

'Car.' The man's voice seemed to stick in his throat, as if his mouth was so dry he couldn't get the words out. 'Must use your . . . car . . .'

Ryan barred his way. 'No. It's my dad's car.' If this was to be his only opportunity to prove himself that night, then he would seize it. No one was going to take his dad's car.

The man looked weak, but he was desperate. He wouldn't listen. It was as if Ryan hadn't spoken at all. He pushed Ryan aside, hauled open the car door. Ryan tried to grab him. 'No!'

But the man ignored him, slid into the front seat. His dad had left the keys in the ignition and the man turned the engine on. Still Ryan tried to pull him out. The man only pushed him again, and Ryan fell away from the car. Then he was gone, and Ryan could only watch and feel, once more, that he had let his dad down.

The sounds were diminishing and Lenny drew his hands away from his ears. The noises had been deafening, sounds that frightened him. Now he must find the boy again, for the Reaper would be angry at him if he failed. He would climb down through the pipes and search him out. He opened his eyes and there below him he saw movement. At first he thought it was the boy, and that he might leap on him and catch him at last. Good thing he waited. The movements were sinuous and slow, but he knew how fast they could move when they wanted.

The Guardians were taking over the tunnels. Why had the Reaper freed them? To get the boy, of course. And they would. No trouble. There was nowhere for the boy to run to get away from them. Lenny would stay up here, safe. The Guardians couldn't get him here.

I looked up. Could I make the pipes? This time there was no handy step for me to rest my foot on. And they were coming ever closer. *Get out of this one, Ram!*

I leapt for the pipes. But my hands slipped on the slimy surface.

The alligators saw me. It was as if those eyes honed in on me. Were they hungry? I bet they were kept that way, just in case. In an instant they would be within striking distance. *Take the chance, Ram. Leap for it again.*

And I did. They were almost on me when I threw myself up, grabbed the pipe with both hands, willed myself to cling there. I swung my legs up too, tucked my toes behind the pipes, prayed I could hold on. I dared not look below me, but I could feel them, hear them. Hear their snapping. I cried out – couldn't stop myself. I had never been so afraid. I saw out of the corner of my eye the jaws open wide, waiting for me to drop in. They scrabbled about on the damp floor, tails cracking together. Help me! But no one would. No one could. Once again, I had to help myself.

I felt my hands slipping, and I was too afraid to try to get a better grip in case I slipped altogether. I was shaking, trembling, heard my teeth chatter. They were fighting over me, as if they knew I couldn't hold on much longer, as if they only had to wait and I would fall into their open mouths.

I prayed for someone to save me.

59

It had been a stroke of genius on his part to bring the Guardians here. None of his specimens had dared escape once they saw what patrolled the corridors outside their cells. Of course, he, the Reaper, couldn't take all the credit. He had got the idea on a visit to Florida, talking to one of the sewer workers there. He had asked why the man needed to carry a gun.

'Need it for them big old 'gators we find lurking in the sewers,' the man had told him. 'When one of them rushes you, gun's the only protection you got.'

And wasn't this bunker just like a sewer?

Of course, they'd had a bit of trouble bringing them down here . . . well, Lenny had. But it had been well worth the effort. And the little touch of phosphorus gave them an eerie glow that made them even scarier.

He wanted them to get the boy. Because of him, all his hard work was lost. He would have to start again.

Yes, he wanted them to get the boy.

The Dark Man burst round the corner, stopped dead – couldn't take in what he was seeing: the boy dangling from the pipes, nightmare creatures snapping at him, trying to bring him down. What the hell had been going on in this place? He stepped back automatically, tracked into Gallacher, who saw them too and let out a yell.

The creatures swivelled their huge heads round towards the two men, suddenly aware of their presence. He was so close to the boy . . . but that yell had given the boy the chance to pull himself out of reach, and now the creatures were turning, lumbering towards him and Gallacher. He knew how fast they could move, accelerating in seconds when they were after prey.

'Run!' he yelled.

The boy wouldn't get far. He would still have him.

I couldn't believe it. The Dark Man had saved me! I had prayed for a saviour . . . and it had been him. I saw him speed off with Ryan's dad, didn't care if they were caught by the alligators, hot in pursuit. I dropped to the ground, couldn't have held on a second longer. My arms ached with pain. Which way to go now? I saw the Dark Man and Gallacher turn the corner, the creatures after them. But they were running the wrong way, away from the opening. Now was my chance. I could surely make it to the hatch. Escape. I drew in a deep breath. I wasn't out of danger yet, but for another minute, at least, I was still alive. *One more minute of life is life*. I clung to that thought, knowing that I could, at least, find my way out of here better than they could.

Lenny lay along the pipes, saw the men running, racing; saw the panic on their faces. He knew what was behind them. Knew it. He watched with growing excitement, safe up there. Always safe. The Reaper had taught him how to be safe; had taught him what to do about the Guardians if they were ever unleashed and had to be controlled. For the moment he watched and saw with amusement the expressions on the men's faces as they ran. The Guardians were fast. It had always fascinated him just how fast they could suddenly move. They would surely catch them. But the men had pace too, and agility. They dodged and leapt like athletes. This was no fun. He wanted down. He wanted to find the boy. He wanted to please the Reaper. Those men didn't matter. The Reaper would want the boy caught. He would want the Guardians controlled. Lenny scrambled along the pipes after the men, his eye clear on the Guardians, waiting for his moment.

Enough of this, the Dark Man thought. His eyes scanned the green gloom as he ran, saw the open cell door ahead. 'Get them in there.'

'How?' Gallacher said.

'Bait!' And the Dark Man leapt into the cell.

The alligators didn't waste a second either – they were in there after him. But he had no intention of being any-thing's dinner. He almost danced round the walls, saw the camp bed in the darkness, leapt on it while the alligators, just a little slower now, came in behind him. And once they were in, he was on his way out, stepping on their hard backs, keeping his nerve – fast, quick, deadly, just as his training had taught him to be – and he was out. Gallacher was waiting, ready to run again.

'If only we could get the door closed,' he said. But there was no time. He had to get the boy.

Lenny could see that the Guardians were there inside the cell. The man had led them inside and then leapt out. Lenny was impressed by how fast he moved. But hadn't the Reaper told him that the Guardians must be kept inside the cell to keep them all safe? Control was the key. Lenny looked down at the levers on the wall. He saw the lever that would shut tight the cell door. He had seen the Reaper use it so many times. He had shown Lenny how to use it too.

Now was his moment – to keep the Guardians safe, and to save himself. And to make the Reaper proud of him. He squeezed through the narrow slit to the floor, grabbed the lever and yanked it down.

Nothing happened. Lenny's hand began to shake. It was the wrong lever. He had closed the outer hatch. Why could he never do anything right?

He looked again. This time he found the right handle. He was sure of it now.

Lenny could see that the Guardians were there inside

The Reaper had been surprised when the big man had raced into the cell where he had been keeping out of sight, waiting for Lenny, for the boy. He was even more amazed at the speed of him leaping back out.

He knew the Guardians had come in and were here in the cell with him, but he could leap out too, lock them inside. The Guardians were no threat to him.

Nothing was a threat to him.

He closed his eyes for a moment, imagined that leap in his mind. That one long leap to freedom and the green light.

And when he opened his eyes, he saw the doors begining to close.

The shock of it turned his old man legs to jelly. He squeaked. He whimpered. He had hesitated a second too long. The green light was disappearing. Its narrow beam growing thinner and thinner, and then, with a final clatter of steel . . . all was black.

Here in the cell, total blackness. Silence.

The blood from the wound on his face dripped to the ground.

The Guardians heard it, caught the scent of blood.

And all the Reaper could hear was the swish-swish as the Guardians moved towards him.

And they were hungry.

60

As I ran I heard the slamming of a cell door. I didn't hesitate for a second, could hear the sound of running feet somewhere, gaining on me, and I knew the Dark Man and Ryan's dad were still there, coming after me. The alligators hadn't got them after all.

I reached the end of the corridor, saw the ladder and threw myself at it. If I could get out this way I might be able to lose myself in the dark. My hand slipped and I almost fell, but I gripped again and pulled myself up.

The hatch was closed. I pushed at it, thumped on it, hoping someone up there might hear me and pull it open. But we were sealed in silence down here. I had no time to wait. They were coming closer.

I looked down at the dark water. Only one other way to freedom – or to certain death? Did it matter now? They were almost upon me. I had made it once. Couldn't be lucky enough to make it again.

But I had one thing that gave me at least a fighting chance. I knew where the murky water below led. I knew the strength of the current.

They didn't. Was that enough?

I had no time to think. I shook with the fear of what I was about to do.

Footsteps pounding closer. A second to choose.

I dived.

He heard the splash. The hatch was closed. The boy had no other option but to jump into the water.

Gallacher stopped, breathless. 'There's nowhere for him to go,' he said.

The Dark Man shook his head. 'He's been here before. If he's gone in there, there has to be a way out. And he knows it.'

It didn't matter if there was or not; if the boy had gone down into that dark water, then he was going to follow him.

'I'm coming too,' Gallacher said.

The Darkman didn't want him to. The boy was his. But Gallacher was in the water the instant before him. He heard him gasp as the cold hit him. Then Gallacher was under.

The Dark Man dived in.

The ice-cold water seemed to freeze my blood. I held my breath as I felt above for that opening to the roof. What if I couldn't feel it this time? What if the water had risen and now there was no life-giving air for me to breathe?

No, there must be. I had to be staying alive for some reason. Behind me, though I could not hear them, I knew they would be there, edging ever closer, like death itself.

Suddenly, my hand touched air and then rock. I moved up. Centimetres of air – only enough to open my mouth, breathe, take in deep gulps, feeling my path along the roof.

Any second now I would feel the tug of the current. I tried to brace myself, prepare my body so I wouldn't be taken by surprise this time.

But no one could completely brace themselves for its power. Like some beast reaching out for its prey, I felt my ankle being gripped. I took one final long, deep pull of air, and then I was drawn under with a speed I couldn't believe.

He found the air pocket, grabbed at Gallacher, hauled him towards it too. One small pocket of air and the boy knew where it was. Yet he was gone. There must be more.

Gallacher drew in the air. 'Where does this lead to?'

The Dark Man didn't know the answer to that. All he knew was that the boy didn't die easily. He could survive more than this.

'Where does this lead –' Gallacher began again, but he didn't finish. Suddenly, his head was gone, pulled down as if something had grabbed his legs.

It was coming for the Dark Man too. He sucked in as much air as he could and felt the current suddenly drag him under.

I twirled and twisted in the fast-moving water, my only thought now to keep some air in my lungs, stay alive, and then . . . I pushed the image of that dark hellhole out of my mind. *One more minute of life is life.*

I was still alive.

Just.

Light.

I could see it through the water.

Dawn's early light. Morning. I was racing towards it. Pounded against stone and rock, I began to grab at whatever I could. Seconds in the open air and I would hit the waterfall. Down I would go, plunging like a stone. I tried to kill my speed. I gripped grass but could hold on to nothing. Going too fast.

And then I was out. At least if I was about to die, I wanted to die in the open air, in the dawn. Streaks of orange lit the sky, and at last I could breathe, gulping in water and air, heading for the falls.

They were behind me. I could hear them, plunging even faster than me. They would reach me soon. I dared not turn, had to keep myself alive. I gripped at the grass again, but my fingers only slipped through.

I rolled and twisted. Any moment now would come that almost vertical drop down into the Doom. I had to get out of the water. I had to keep away from the Dark Man.

I had to live!

61

FRIDAY

Open air. A waterfall. The boy a hand's breadth in front of him. If he could reach out now he would have him. But he couldn't reach out, not for the boy. He was clinging on to anything to stop himself from going over.

Gallacher was tumbling out of the hillside as fast as he was, suddenly lifted over the ridge of the tunnel and down again, like some crazy white-water ride.

The Dark Man was turning, his body hitting rock. He grabbed at the bank, felt his fingers claw through mud. Then, just when he thought he could go no faster, the water ride tipped over almost vertically. He yelled out, saw the boy below him. He was being tossed and turned like a twig. For a second, the Dark Man caught a glimpse of a black hole far below, where the waterfall suddenly disappeared in an angry white foam. He saw now why the boy was going crazy for a hold of something. He did too: grass, rocks, anything to stop him going down. His hand snapped hold of a branch of a tree hanging over the bank. He held it, clung to it. Gallacher must have seen the drop too. The Dark Man saw his eyes, wide with alarm, dart from the water's edge to the branch, judging the distance, desperate to get a hold.

The Dark Man clung tight. Now his feet were firm on earth, on rock. He pulled himself up, using all his will to keep that hold. The boy, centimetres below him, had gripped on to another branch, but his hold was slipping.

I saw the Dark Man pulling his long frame up and on to the bank, but I was going down, couldn't hold on much longer. Ryan's dad caught in the torrent was gripping fiercely on to a branch, but I could see it bending, ready to snap. I could see that he, like me, would soon plunge – I glanced down, no, not there! The thought of being lost in that blackness terrified me more than almost anything I could think of . . . almost anything except being in the clutches of the Dark Man.

Maybe this was the way I could win, by letting go, by watching his face as he saw that I was to be lost to him for ever.

Ryan's dad held out his hand to the Dark Man – his friend, his companion – and the Dark Man reached out to him.

My fingers were being torn from the branch. No one to save me.

I closed my eyes. I would not watch the black hole coming closer. I would try to die first, drown.

Seconds before my death, it was my hand that was gripped. My hand, my arm, and I felt myself being dragged out of the water. I opened my eyes. The Dark Man had me. The Dark Man had saved me.

I heard a yell, a woeful scream. One I will never forget. And I turned and watched as Ryan's dad lost his hold, his fingers frantically searching for another, finding none. The foam seemed to lift him up, turn him round, and carry him, as if in some terrible act of sacrifice, down and down. I watched his eyes, full of dread, as he plunged towards the edge of the waterfall, still trying to scrabble for a hold – but it was no use. He knew it. In those last seconds, he knew death was hurtling towards him. He could see the betrayal in the Dark Man's eyes too.

His wail was long and painful. My last sight of him – will I ever forget it? – just those terrified eyes disappearing down into that black hellhole.

The Dark Man pulled me on to the bank beside him. 'Gotcha!'

62

It was over. After all this, he had me. I lay back on the muddy verge and knew it had to be over. The Dark Man loomed above me and looked deep into my eyes.

Had I known him before? I knew I had – had seen visions of him, as a friend, as someone I trusted. Once I had even thought he might be my dad. But who was he? Why did he want me? Maybe now I would find out the truth.

And, as I watched, the Dark Man crumpled. He stumbled to his knees, his eyes glassy, his face white as death. He clutched at his head. Blood trickled through his fingers.

'Run, boy!'

It was Catman. He threw the rock he had hit him with to the ground. 'Run!'

I got to my feet.

'Run!' Catman cried out again.

'Bella,' I said, clutching his sleeve. 'They killed her. Find her body. Please . . .'

Catman nodded, stunned. Then I didn't wait. I ran – only looked back once. The Dark Man would be on his feet soon, would be after me, angry at losing me once more. Catman stood tall, I had never realised just how tall he was, and I ran, ran into the early morning. The orange dawn was streaking the sky, and an energy I never knew that I had was leaping from me.

Alive, safe, free of him again. And I would stay free. It was a new dawn. And I was still alive.

Ryan sat on the grass, waiting for his dad to come back. Where was he? He had stared at the hatch for such a long time, watching for it to rise again, watching for his dad and the Dark Man to climb through. His dad would tell him that Ram was gone for ever, or they would have Ram with them, so they could find out what he knew. The secret.

So where were they?

In the distance he could hear the wail of a police car. The last thing his dad would want was the police involved. Should he go home? They would want to know why he, Ryan, was here. They would want to interrogate him – about his dad's car, his whereabouts – and Ryan wouldn't know how to answer them. Maybe he should just go home.

His mum would be worried. She'd know what to do. She was one of them too.

Ryan stood up, took one last look at the hatch. His dad would be OK. His dad was always OK. *We are special people*, he had said, and Ryan believed him. His dad would want him to go home.

He turned and began to walk down the hill towards the town.

Catman knew he wouldn't stand a chance if this Dark Man stood and fought. He looked as if he could snap his neck like a chicken's if he wanted. But Catman had to keep him there a while, give the boy a fighting chance to get away. He would hit him again if he had to, wished he had it in his power to kill him. But he knew he could never kill anyone. The ability to kill wasn't in most good people. Maybe that was their weakness, he thought. Or maybe it was their strength.

He stood back as the long, lean man got to his unsteady feet. His eyes were dark with anger. Catman ran at him, took him by surprise, nearly had him on the ground again, but the man was quick, well trained. He almost lifted Catman off his feet, threw him away from him. He didn't want to fight, he wanted away, after the boy. Not enough time, Catman thought and he was on him again. This time he hit him hard, rammed his head against the man's ribs. They both fell back, rolled on the ground. He could hear the police cars racing closer. They both could. The man tensed, threw him from him. Catman fell so hard against the rocks he almost lost consciousness. If he'd had time this Dark Man would have finished him off. But the police were too close. He looked at Catman as though he was dirt beneath him, and then he was gone.

Had he given the boy enough time?

That boy?

Yes. That boy would make it, he was sure of it.

Catman took a moment to get his breath, and then he got to his feet and walked slowly back towards the lost people.

63

I stole a ride in the back of an old farm truck. Didn't know where it was going, didn't care. I was wet and shivering with cold. But I was away from the Dark Man again.

I needed dry clothes, somewhere to sleep, something to eat. Nothing worried me. I would find a way to get them. I thought of Catman saving me, a life in his eyes I hadn't seen before. I thought of Bella and I wanted to cry.

I even thought of Ryan, finding out that his father was dead.

I patted my pockets and pulled out the photograph again, tried to make out the faces. It was damp, the figures slightly blurred now. But still I could see clearly the Dark Man, a soldier, sleeves rolled up, somewhere in the desert. Ryan's dad too, and I tried to blot out the image of his eyes as he plunged to his death – had to look away, found myself almost crying. He had been Ryan's dad, the dad he loved, and now he was gone. I hoped Ryan never found out how.

It took me a moment before I could look back at the photograph – to study the man in the middle. I knew I had seen him before . . . but where? Was he someone from my past, and if he was, why weren't flashing images of him rushing towards me? I closed my eyes. Concentrated. All I could see was another photo. A photo I had seen on a news website on Bella's computer, and with it, a headline.

DISGRUNTLED CIVIL SERVANT
THE LONE BOMBER

And my mind exploded.

This was the man who had been haunting my memory since I'd woken up without one in that tower block a few weeks ago.

He had been no lone bomber, though. He had been part of a conspiracy, and the Dark Man and Ryan's dad were all part of it too.

And so was I.

I knew it now.

I knew something else too. My name did mean something. I just didn't know what. I remembered the look on Ryan's dad's face when Ryan had called me Ram.

Shock. Realisation.

I thought I had chosen my name at random, but I was wrong. Ram was from my memory.

I tried to work it out.

Ryan's family were here. Bella had called them a 'sleeper cell'. She had said that something was coming. Something big. Something so big it would change the world?

We'll be the new law and order soon, Ryan had said. And I imagined the Dark Man taking over, and the shivers I felt were not from the cold.

And I could stop it all. But how? Who could I tell? Who could I trust? Bella had worked for the government. So did the Dark Man. I could trust no one.

So how was I ever going to find out what all this was about?

And it came to me in an instant. The Dark Man had been following me, finding me wherever I was. Now I was about to turn the tables.

From now on, I was going to follow the Dark Man.

To find out more about the

author of *Nemesis* and her books

visit

www.macphailbooks.com